"*Pandora's Key* is Greek mythology with a suspenseful, modern twist. This story hooked me from chapter one, and then again, and again with each consecutive chapter. Evangeline (heroine) is super cool… a seemingly normal girl thrust into a freaky, twisted, almost unbelievable adventure. Except it's written in such a way that it feels like it could really happen. You won't put this one down…I didn't. Can't wait for the next story in the trilogy!"

—MythGal (5 stars, Amazon)

"I'm a big fan of mythology, so I was intrigued by the opening chapters and immediately I was hooked. This book is wildly entertaining, imaginative and creative—the twisting plot propels the reader to the end. It's perfect for teens but also for adults who enjoy a great fantasy with lots of symbolism and interesting characters. Definitely worth the read!"

—KM (5 stars, Amazon)

"I simply couldn't put *Pandora's Key* down. It was a pleasure to read such a beautifully written novel in this genre of coming-of-age fantasy thrillers. It's a bit like Dan Brown meets Twilight with a mythological twist. I would recommend this book to teenagers and adults alike who appreciate strong heroines, suspense and unexpected twists."

—A McKenna (5 stars, Amazon)

"I really loved this book! While the story is supernatural, it's believable. It's a page turner—fast paced and never boring or drawn out. I'm ready for Book #2! Hope it comes out soon!"

—Lisa A. Mitchell (5 stars, Amazon)

"I couldn't put down *Pandora's Key*. It's the kind of book you try to avoid the ending of, so you can just keep reading it. I loved this book and I would definitely recommend it to friends."

—Emily Whitfield (5 stars, Amazon)

"*Pandora's Key* is a delightfully magical story about two separate peoples' lives and how they end up intertwining. Once the background is established…the book becomes spellbinding. The words just flow! From young teens through adults, all aspects of the story are clearly understandable. The Greek mythology in the prologue serves as a hint of where this inspiration began. I am a retired educator and I loved this book!"

—Peter (5 stars, Amazon)

"When I first started to read this book there was no way I was going to put it down. The story sucks you in and when something sad or scary happens you feel the emotion, too. Pandora's Key has a range of everything, from mystery to romance it creates detail of the characters and you feel like you are there with all of them."

—Lucy B (5 stars, Amazon)

"For any teen that enjoys action, suspense and mythology, *Pandora's Key* is the perfect read. With compassionate characters and exciting plot twists, it truly kept me on the edge of my seat. *Pandora's Key* is action packed, filled with magic, and has just the right amount of romance mixed in to make it a wonderful coming of age tale."

—Abby Dennis (5 stars, Amazon)

"The thing that strikes me most about Pandora's Key is that it's such a sophisticated YA book that I'm 40 and couldn't put it down. Seriously, I read it in three hours and can't wait for the next book in The Key Trilogy. Fischer's debut urban fantasy novel seamlessly blends Greek mythology with a gritty, modern world. There's something for everyone—a teenage girl coming of age and forced to accept a terrible gift and burden; a doctor drowning from loss and struggling to find something to believe in; and an antagonist who is brilliant, desperate and devolves into pure evil. There was enough magic, ancient curses, Gods and Goddesses and powerful talisman to create a story that travels at a breakneck ace. Bravo Nancy Richardson Fischer—now get busy writing the sequel!"

—Ashley Anderson (5 stars, Amazon)

"This story is highly addictive… I must say, I didn't expect to be so emotionally invested in the storyline. I cried, bit my nails down to the cuticle, and held my breath until I simply had to put the book down to find release. But I couldn't keep it down for long, because I simply had to know what would happen next. I'm currently in a state of impatience; anxiously awaiting the sequel in The Key Trilogy."

—Katrina (Kindred Dreamheart, 4 stars, Goodreads)

"I thought [Pandora's Key] was very well written and well thought out. It kept me on the edge of my seat... and stayed on my mind when I had to put it down. An intriguing twist of plots where you were constantly wondering who was friend and who was foe... I really appreciated this unique take on an ancient legend."

—Alison W (4 stars, Goodreads)

"[Pandora's Key] had a complex plot that was woven expertly and subtly. In terms of pace, this book moved very quickly... I thought the characters were fantastic! They were realistic and three-dimensional and I loved learning about them from their own perspective as well as through the eyes of others... I think the real genius with this book lies in the delivery... I will DEFINITELY read the rest of the series! The characters were enthralling, the story fantastically told, and there were lots of twists and unexpected surprises to keep me on my toes! All in all, this makes for a great read! I can't wait for the next book to come out!"

—Jeanette (5 stars, Goodreads)

"I love the Greek mythology. I love the storyline. I love the characters."

—Chey (5 stars, Goodreads)

"I could not put [Pandora's Key] down... It was brilliant... I found myself holding my breath while reading because there were so many twists [and] I didn't know what was going to happen... Nancy is such a great author and she has a way of hooking you to the story... [she] is definitely an author to look out for. Pandora's Key is such a great book and all mythology fans will love it."

—OCD Kay (K-Books, 4 stars, Goodreads)

"From the first page of Pandora's Key, Nancy Richardson Fischer grabs your attention...Every reader will find themselves lost in this book...Fischer successfully captures the readers' attention, with endless action and unusual twists and turns that never let you go."

—Katheryn36 (5 stars, Goodreads)

"Everything about Pandora's Key is intriguing, from the title to the last word."

—Shannon (5 stars, Goodreads)

"Prepare to be disappointed! You are going to want to read the other books in this trilogy and they are not in print yet! This is a story based on Greek mythology with a paranormal flavor... In a field of YA books, this one stands out. It is a refreshing change of pace from vampires. This one is not just another Twilight wannabe!"

—Glenda Christianson (5 stars, Goodreads)

"This book was so fantastic it left my brain paralyzed."

—Emilija (5 stars, Goodreads)

Edition: April 2012

Praise for PANDORA'S KEY

"With vivid imagery, compelling characters and plenty of bursts of action, this first novel weaving mythology and contemporary teenage troubles is thrillingly memorable!

[In] this fresh, intriguing novel, Fischer is clearly laying the groundwork for a trilogy that will successfully continue to bring ancient mythology forward into a modern tale of self discovery…[and] Fischer's fast pacing and numerous plot twists are sure to keep the reader turning the pages…"

—*Kirkus Indie*

"In this inventive debut installment of The Key Trilogy, an Oregon girl's life is uprooted by the discovery of her pivotal role in a prophecy stemming from Greek mythology… Surprising twists add to the story's intrigue. The co-author of several sports autobiographies, Fischer hits her stride in this quick-paced novel."

—*Publishers Weekly*

"Never have I seen a book take over my classroom like this one did... I haven't seen this much enthusiasm since [my] students read The Hunger Games Trilogy... "

—Sandra K. Stiles (5 stars, Amazon)

"In *Pandora's Key* the story of Evangeline moves along quite quickly, a wonderful thing after reading so many books with slow starts. Hearing about the mythology of Pandora and Pandora's Box was a treat. The entire story was well written and there wasn't a dull moment to be found...While this story wrapped up the beginning, there is still so much more that can be had in continuing the series and I would love to see where it goes."

—Jessica for *Book Sake*

"*Pandora's Key* was a wonderful spin on Greek Mythology. The characters were engaging and there were twists and unexpected turns throughout the book."

—The Norman Howard School (5 stars, Amazon)

"A great read for the young to not-so-young readers alike. Fischer has a captivating imagination and wonderful story telling ability. This book will throw you an unexpected twist just when you think you figured it out. I can't wait for the next two!"

—Castine 207 (5 stars, Amazon)

PANDORA'S KEY

PANDORA'S KEY

NANCY RICHARDSON FISCHER

THE KEY TRILOGY • BOOK ONE

This book is for Henry—
my best friend, husband, and partner in adventure and magic.

"We must be willing to let go of the life we planned so as to have the life that is waiting for us."

—*Joseph Campbell*

PROLOGUE

Thousands of years ago the Gods and Goddesses of Mount Olympus created the first woman and named her Pandora. Each God gave Pandora a magical gift. Aphrodite, Goddess of Love and Beauty, bestowed beauty. Poseidon, God of the Sea, bequeathed black pearls so Pandora would never drown. Haephestus, God of Fire and Metalworking, gave Pandora the ability to create reality from imagination. Apollo, God of the Sun and the Arts, granted her musical prowess. Athena, the warrior Goddess, contributed the ability to kill, and Demeter, Goddess of the Harvest, tempered that attribute with healing powers. The Messenger God, Hermes, gave Pandora the trait of cunning.

Not to be outdone, Zeus, King of the Gods, gave Pandora two gifts. First, he endowed her with curiosity. And, second, he gave her an intricately carved gold box that emanated a soft rose-colored glow as a gift for mankind designed to punish them for accepting stolen fire from Mount Olympus. The box was filled with five Furies: Plagues, Natural Disasters, Hatred, Jealousy, and the most horrific fifth Fury, Annihilation. Zeus reasoned that curious Pandora would open the box and the Furies would be released to torment mankind for eternity. He allowed his wife, Hera, Goddess of Women and Marriage, to add Hope to the box before he closed it, because men would need a reason to live once the Furies had been released.

At the last moment, Hades, God of the Underworld, placed a delicate chain around innocent Pandora's neck. Dangling from it was a small key fashioned from iridescent onyx. If curious Pandora was cunning enough to close the box before the most devastating fifth Fury escaped, she could use the key to keep it locked away. The Gods added a few more twists and turns to ensure their amusement and then sent their lovely creation and her poisonous gift down to earth.

Over the ensuing tens-of-centuries, the onyx key was preserved, but all memory of its history and of the box faded until only a handful of people knew the truth. Some of those people were innocents, as Pandora had been. Some were devious and lethal when crossed. And some were evil or simply insane.

CHAPTER ONE

It was a cold May in the Pacific Northwest, but in one backyard bulbs had already pushed through untended soil and opened their petals, revealing cheerful yellow daffodils and snow-white tulips. In adjacent yards, spring flowers had yet to peek out of soil tilled and fertilized by professional gardening services.

Perhaps the early blooms were what made this particular backyard feel bewitched. Or maybe it was the humming-birds, which would not be seen anywhere else in Oregon for several months, hovering over honeysuckle that shouldn't be blooming until July. But the other-worldly effect could simply have been the result of the shadows and weak gleam of moonlight casting a silver net over the premises.

Two men slipped through the backyard's white picket gate. They were dressed in black and wore woolen ski masks that revealed only the drooping hooked nose of the taller one and the almond-shaped eyes of the second, much shorter, but broader, man. The men moved soundlessly to the pale-yellow house, the taller man inserting a thin rod into the seam of the sliding glass door. There was a clicking sound as the lock opened.

The second man slid a compact gun from his side and released the safety. With his free hand he eased the slider open, then hesitated and looked down at his chest where a red flower suddenly bloomed. His knees buckled and the taller man whirled around to help…but it was already too late. The arc of a curved blade caught his neck just below the ski mask and sliced it cleanly, sending up a spray of fine blood. Hands caught both men before they hit the ground. Silently, they were dragged away.

The only witness to the bloody scene was an orange and white tabby who sat unblinking in the picture window.

CHAPTER TWO

Evangeline climbed a rickety wooden ladder into the hayloft. She wore a cotton nightgown she'd never seen before—ivory-colored with tiny pink roses, long enough to brush the tops of her bare feet…except they weren't her feet, because they were too small and delicate and the nails were painted cherry-red.

When she reached the loft, she found a lantern on the floor. Raising the glass top, she lit the wick with a match she hadn't known she carried, and then turned the brass knob. The lantern glowed, illumining lazy dust motes, bales of yellowed hay, and a thick rope coiled in the corner.

Evangeline tossed the free end of the rope over a rafter. She braced herself, leaned out from the ladder, and grabbed the dangling rope. Slowly her hands, which were not her hands because there was a pear-shaped diamond ring on the left ring finger, fashioned the end of the rope into a noose. *I don't know how to make a noose,* Evangeline thought as she slid it over her head and tightened it around her neck.

Evangeline watched her pale feet shuffle along the uneven, slatted floor toward the edge of the hayloft. Her pulse raced. *This isn't happening.* But she could smell the thick, cloying sweetness of the hay. *This can't be real.* But she felt a splinter from the rough wood bite into her heel. *Stop!* And then she stepped into space, stomach hurtling into her mouth—terror numbing her body—rope tightening—legs kicking...

. . .

Evangeline struggled to consciousness. Her heart thudded painfully and a thin film of sweat coated her face. She looked down—blue flannel PJ's. No diamond ring. Size ten feet— no nail polish—poking from beneath her down comforter. Her fingers slid along the smooth skin of her neck, feeling for rope burns—none.

"It was only a nightmare," Evangeline whispered. But it had felt incredibly real and it took some time to slow her pulse and banish the strange dream from her mind. *And that's all it was,* she told herself, sitting up and wiping her face— *just a stupid dream.*

Rolling out of bed, she shuffled down the hall. She walked through her mom's bedroom with its queen-sized bed covered with the hand-made quilt of yellow and orange squares that her mother's agent, Samantha, had given her. She side-stepped the rocking chair and her mom's beat-up guitar, and passed an antique bureau topped by an oval mirror whose gold border framed glass hazy with age.

Stepping through the open door of the bathroom, Evangeline watched her mom brushing her teeth. Olivia Theopolis, dressed in a paint-splattered T-shirt and worn Levis, had probably already been working for hours on the new painting she'd refused to show her daughter. Evangeline couldn't help noticing that her white-blonde hair was perfectly smooth and straight compared to her own shoulder-length locks that always curled out of control. Self-conscious, she tried to press her hair down and her mom noticed her rumpled reflection in the mirror.

"H-phy-b-fdy," she said, before spitting out a mouthful of toothpaste. "Evangel—" Suddenly, her mom's knees buckled and she grabbed the edge of the pedestal sink to keep from falling. She leaned forward, peering into the porcelain bowl.

"Blood," she whispered, confused. And then she looked into the mirror, mouth open wide, shaking fingers running over her teeth. "My teeth—"

The back of Evangeline's neck prickled. "Mom?"

Her mother turned—her flawless skin pale. "I don't understand. My teeth are falling out and there's blood in the sink."

A chill slithered down Evangeline's spine as she walked to the sink and peered nervously into it. The porcelain was pure white with a few rivulets of the aqua-colored toothpaste her mom had spit out moments ago. *No blood—no blood anywhere. What is she talking about?*

Evangeline released the breath she'd been holding. "Mom, I don't understand—there's nothing in the sink but toothpaste." She looked at her mom's frightened face and suddenly she was scared. "Your teeth are all there," Evangeline said and gently turned her mother around to look.

Slowly the color came back to the woman's cheeks and she was again Evangeline's beautiful, young mother. The mom all the boys in her class stared at when she picked up E from school. The one who made them all whisper about how the apple had fallen so far from the tree. And it had. Olivia had bowed pink lips, stunning sky-blue eyes, the body of a gazelle. Evangeline was a giraffe—long neck, gangly limbs, eerie blue-black eyes, and an impossibly wide mouth.

"E, I'm sorry," her mom said. "I must've still been half-asleep."

Evangeline tried to shake off the sticky residue of fear. "It's okay, but I think—I mean, I don't want to bum you out, but it's not the first—"

"I'm fine," her mom interrupted. "Really, I just need more sleep." She smiled and took her daughter's hand, leading her out of the bathroom.

"Where are we going?"

"Your room." Her mom flashed a secretive smile. "Check under your pillow."

Evangeline ran down the hallway. She raced to her bed and tossed one of her pillows onto the floor—nothing. Beneath the second pillow, which was still indented from her head, was a gift-wrapped box.

"Happy sixteenth birthday, Evangeline, my not-so-little-girl."

Grinning, Evangeline picked up the package, which was wrapped in hand-painted purple-flowered paper that must've taken her mom hours to make. For a moment, as she ripped open the paper, she thought she smelled floral perfume, but neither of them wore perfume, preferring the fresh scent of soap. Evangeline hoped that this gift was the iPad she'd been wanting so badly. Inside the box was a second box, also wrapped in hand-crafted paper decorated with small white and yellow daisies. The cloying sweetness of torn stems seemed to fill the air as Evangeline tore open the paper. *Maybe*, she thought, *your sense of imagination gets better with age. Or maybe mom and I are both losing it.*

Not that her mom was crazy or anything. It was just that, for the past month some weird stuff had been happening. As far as Evangeline could recall, her mom had never had a cold, let alone a headache. But lately she'd been having migraines that made her too nauseated to eat. And then there were the dreams that punctuated some nights with screams so loud Evangeline had to rush to her mom's bed to wake her. Her mom never remembered the nightmares, which seemed weird considering how violently she reacted to them. Two nights ago Evangeline had found her mom sitting on the bedroom floor holding her hairbrush.

"What're you doing, mom?"

"I can't brush my hair. It keeps falling out." Olivia had stared up at her daughter like a little kid, eyes brimming with tears. And then she'd pointed to what she'd said were bare spots on her scalp.

Evangeline had helped her mom to her feet and led her to the mirror where they'd examined her mom's hair together. It still fell in a perfect sheet of platinum to the edge of her square jaw. Her mom had smiled and said she must've fallen asleep getting ready for bed and had a bad dream. "At least this time I remembered it," Olivia said with a brittle laugh.

"Yeah, that's something," Evangeline had replied, but what she'd really wanted to say was: Please stop freaking me out. This woman who'd never been sick couldn't imagine that something might be wrong with her. Evangeline didn't think it was anything serious, but the idea of her mother losing it in any way made her feel off-balance, like the world was threatening to start spinning in the wrong direction.

Evangeline tossed the daisy wrapping paper only to find a still smaller box covered in paper dotted with hand-painted orange, yellow, and red trees. For a brief moment, their leaves fluttered in an invisible breeze. Evangeline quickly looked away and tore off the wrapping, opening the box. Inside was a violet-colored silk bag. The bag gave Evangeline a strange sense of déjà vu even though she'd never seen it before.

Easing open the drawstring, she spilled the contents onto her palm. It was a necklace. The delicate silver chain gave off a soft glow. Dangling from it was a small black key carved from some luminous stone. Evangeline again felt a sense of déjà vu.

"Mom?" she asked, glancing at her mother's bare neck and then meeting her eyes.

"It's a tradition in our family, E. I don't know who started it, but my mother, and her mother before her and on and on gave this necklace to each of their daughters on their sixteenth birthday—or so the story goes."

"I've never seen you take it off." Evangeline traced the outline of the key in her palm.

"I never have."

"But you *love* this necklace."

Her mom smiled. "That's why I want you to have it." She took the necklace from Evangeline, undid the clasp, and placed it around her neck.

"Do you know what the key was made to unlock?"

"I asked my mother the same thing, but she had no idea. Maybe it was just meant to be pretty."

Evangeline looked down at the key resting between her collarbones. Heat seemed to emanate from it and the feeling washed over her skin like warm water, along with a tingling sensation and a strange shift—a feeling of total comfort that she could only describe as her body finally fitting into its own skin. *Stop imagining things.* But there was no question that the key somehow belonged around her neck, along with the accompanying sense of warmth.

Evangeline looked into the mirror above her dresser. When she was younger, she'd dress in her mom's clothes, blur her eyes, and pretend she was the glamorous Olivia. And suddenly now with the key her mother had always worn resting around her own neck, it somehow made her feel like she looked different, better—well, less like Big Bird. At least her eyes didn't seem quite so enormous and she could differentiate the gloomy-blue of her irises from her black pupils, which looked iridescent. *Is this possible?* The smooth black key appeared almost liquid against her pale skin—fluid and incandescent.

"Thanks so much mom—I really, really love it."

Her mother pulled Evangeline into a hug, holding on for a few seconds too long. "Good. You deserve it."

Pulling free from the embrace, Evangeline headed toward the hall. "How about I make us waffles," she offered, because when they'd hugged, she'd felt her mother's sharp shoulder blades and couldn't help but notice that her mom's jeans hung off jutting hipbones. *When did she lose so much weight?*

They made breakfast together in the cozy kitchen of the bungalow they shared with their orange and white cat, Jasmine. They moved through their tasks, making coffee, pouring OJ, cutting grapefruit—in the seamless rhythm of two people who had forever shared their lives.

"Yuck," Evangeline said, pointing to the sliding glass door that led out into their backyard. It was splattered with what looked like dried blood.

"Must've been a bird," her mother said, frowning, because she was a freak about loving animals, even mice. She pulled the slider open and looked down in the grass. No bird. "Well, either Jasmine got the poor thing or it flew away." She turned to the tabby, scratching behind her ears. "Which is it, Jas?"

Jasmine looked over at Evangeline without blinking. "If she knows, she's not telling," Evangeline said. She gave her mother the first waffle, poured batter on the griddle to make another, and then bent down to look at the bottom of her foot because it was stinging. "Huh."

"What?"

Evangeline peered closer. "I just have something in my heel…got it." She pulled out a rough, wood splinter—which was weird because the floors in their house were polished bamboo.

CHAPTER THREE

Malledy shifted on the crinkly white paper-covered exam table so he could see Mount Hood out of the tenth floor window. It wasn't awe-inspiring like the mountains around his home, but it was a jagged symbol, at least to him, of hope.

Malledy had come to Portland, Oregon, for two reasons. The first and most important reason was to meet with Dr. Aali. One of the leaders in his field, Dr. Aali was extremely busy, so even after countless scans, blood draws and myriad tests, Malledy had been forced to nervously wait seven weeks for a face-to-face meeting.

The second reason Malledy had come to Portland was to acquire an artifact for a client. He'd not yet told Juliette about the assignment nor that he was getting close to finding the ancient talisman. This acquisition might be his last success and he wanted to surprise Juliette—give her a moment of joy and pride, should Dr. Aali prove to be a literal dead-end.

"Que penses-tu?" Juliette asked.

Malledy turned to face his mentor, trying not to notice how the past four months had aged her. There were gray strands in her auburn hair and deep lines around her intelligent lime-green eyes. She was only forty-four, but today she looked sixty—and scared. For a split-second Malledy was annoyed that he needed to worry about Juliette when he was the one truly suffering. "I was thinking about home," Malledy said, trying to smile reassuringly because none of this was Juliette's fault.

"We can go back there soon."

"Do you think my mother knew that I'd get sick?"

"Non, mon cher. I think she left you because she could not be a mother." Juliette had long ago told Malledy that he should accept that he would never know anything about his biological parents. There simply was no information—no leads to follow—because Malledy had been abandoned as an infant on the doorstep of Castle Aertz, high in the mountains of northeast Italy.

For a brief time when he was nine, Malledy had sought to learn more about his birth mother. He'd questioned people living in the mountain villages closest to the castle, and searched hundreds of parish records for leads. In addition he'd badgered every occupant of Castle Aertz for memories of his arrival but found that a baby abandoned on a doorstep had left little impression and was seen only as a momentary distraction. It became clear that the trail leading to his birth mother was ice cold and Malledy had been forced to swallow his desire and move on.

Malledy looked down at his right hand—it was flopping on his thigh like a weak fish. The current diagnosis for his tremors was "chorea," which basically meant uncontrolled, involuntary movement. He was taking Paroxetine—a tranquilizer to quell the spasms. It was obvious that whatever was wrong with him was getting worse and he needed a higher dose of the drug. In the meantime, if he gripped something when the spasms hit, or crammed his hands into his pockets, he could still the tremors, which so far were the only outward signs of his illness.

"Would you have wanted a different life?" Juliette asked, holding tightly to Malledy's right hand until the spasm relented.

Malledy gave the answer he knew Juliette wanted to hear. "Of course not." The voice in his head said something different: *I would've liked a choice.* Malledy had grown up the only child within the castle. The original owner of the castle, Baron Aertz, had been a scholar in the 1600's who was obsessed with uncovering the mysteries of the world. He'd bought the remote castle and created a clandestine Order called the "Archivists." Those men and women worked in secret for patrons who included a King, a handful of Popes, and other nameless powerful men and women all of whom had three things in common: great wealth, the ability to locate the well-hidden Archivists, and the intelligence to keep the Archivists' secret. Telling tales about the Order meant certain death no matter how rich or important the client might have believed himself to be.

Archivists were recruited for their brilliance and not allowed to have children, who would both distract them and make them soft. They worshipped the God of Knowledge and there were no rules save that the end always justified whatever means necessary to acquire a priceless morsel of information or talisman. Malledy had been the only exception to the Archivists' policy of no children and he was grateful that for some reason they'd decided to allow him to stay at the castle until his tenth birthday. If he'd not proven himself worthy to become one of them by then, he would have been removed.

No one ever defined "removed" for Malledy. But given the secrecy surrounding the Archivists, he'd come to understand that it meant not leaving a young boy alive to talk about a hidden castle high in the Dolomite Mountains containing discoveries powerful enough to topple governments, religions and the very definition of Gods.

Most of his life, Malledy now realized, he'd felt like he was part of a giant chess game, moved around at random by the Archivists. For brief moments, he was allowed to be the player—the hand that shifted certain pieces—instead of a pawn. But those moments were mostly an illusion because the Archivists ultimately made the rules that governed the game and his only choice was to either play by them or be knocked off the board. And now? Now an even more potent force had taken charge of his life and he was at its mercy.

"Thank you, Juliette," Malledy said softly.

"For what?" she asked, shifting her lithe frame to a more comfortable position on the vinyl chair.

"For being my mentor." Juliette had raised Malledy, taught him six languages, and instilled in him the desire to learn more on his own. She's made certain he could debate in ancient Greek, grasp advanced physics, navigate philosophy, and understand complex scientific principles. She had shown him how to dig into any field and parse through thousands of pages of research that might include paintings on cave walls, stolen diaries, and symbols thousands of years old burned into animal hides. She'd been a surrogate mother, tucking him into bed each night and comforting him when he was afraid. Most importantly, Juliette had given Malledy the skills to ultimately find and acquire artifacts for clients so that he might be able to save his own life when his tenth birthday tolled—six long years ago now.

There was a knock on the exam room door. "*Entrée*," Juliette called, and Dr. Aali walked in carrying Malledy's thick medical chart.

Dr. Aali was a skinny man with rectangular glasses too wide for his narrow face. He was only five-foot-four and with his wiry gray-hair looked like a wise, old man in a child's body. He shook Juliette's hand and then patted Malledy on the shoulder. "Nice to see you," he said, sitting down on a stool and rolling forward until he was perched in the space between Malledy and Juliette.

"You've reviewed my MRIs and the new tests?" Malledy asked.

Dr. Aali nodded and opened Malledy's file, scanning it quickly. "Your original physician, Dr. Cantori, diagnosed you with Huntington's disease four months ago based on a genetic test combined with emerging symptoms. But your own research led you to believe you're too young to contract the disease so you came to me for a second opinion."

"That's right." Malledy nodded. "Symptoms usually occur after age thirty-five. In addition, I've had none of the typical warning signs that usually accompany the disease." His heart was beating so hard against his chest that the sensation was painful. *This is what hope feels like.*

"Yes," Dr. Aali said, momentarily distracted as he flipped through his notes. "It's always important to get another opinion—especially when facing this sort of diagnosis."

"Has there been some mistake?" Juliette asked, leaning forward, her hands gripping the edge of the chair. Again Malledy felt irritated. Juliette's fear and need to help both embarrassed him and made him feel guilty. *She cares,* Malledy reminded himself. *She's the only one who ever has.*

Dr. Aali met Malledy's gaze with compassionate brown eyes. "I'm very sorry," he said.

Malledy's stomach cramped violently, and then dropped. His body felt unbearably heavy, weighed down by those three words: I'm very sorry. Malledy had known, hadn't he? Of course he had. After all, his fellow Archivists considered him a genius, and they, themselves, had staggering IQs. Strange, Malledy thought, how he'd spent his entire life unemotionally evaluating facts but when they were personal he'd lost all perspective. *Why did Juliette allow me on this wild goose chase? Because she didn't want to see clearly either.*

"The original diagnosis was correct," Dr. Aali continued. "You have early onset Huntington's disease. While it's rare in a teenager, it's not unheard of. And it progresses much more rapidly in the young. Unfortunately, despite my own and others' research, we still have no cure for the disease."

Dr. Aali closed Malledy's file. "You are clearly a thoughtful young man. I'm going to be straight with you because knowing what to expect will make this process easier. Your chorea will lead to weakened muscles until you'll be unable to walk, talk, or swallow. At some point, the disease will attack your brain causing hallucinations, delusions, and violent outbursts."

Dr. Aali took off his glasses and folded them. "Malledy, you and your mother will need to prepare for the latter stages of this disease because you'll require full-time care. There are also groups that can provide counseling and I'll prescribe drugs to ease the process."

Ease the process—he means drugs to help me die. For a split-second Malledy imagined swinging his right fist and connecting with Dr. Aali's stubby nose, watching the blood splatter across the exam room's bright walls. *This isn't a violent outburst. This is a normal reaction to a horrific death sentence.*

"I don't want to take any more drugs until I need them," Malledy said with forced calm, trying to ignore the fact that Juliette was crying. "Can we increase the dosage of Paroxetine?" The doctor nodded.

Kneeling beside Juliette's chair, Malledy said gently, "It's okay—it was a long shot. We'll get through this together." *Don't make this any worse. Please stop crying.*

Malledy stood and reached out to shake Dr. Aali's hand, making sure his own grip was firm. "Thank you for your time," he said, his throat tight with emotion.

"I'm honored, young man. Now, I'd like to put you on a specific diet. Sometimes eliminating certain food groups can slow the course of the disease. We can monitor you—"

"We'll be going home now," Juliette interrupted, wiping her tears and squaring her shoulders, once again all Archivist.

"No," Malledy said. "I want to stay in town and be treated as an out-patient by Dr. Aali. *For once I'm going to choose how I live...and how I die.*

CHAPTER FOUR

Evangeline and her best friend, Melia, walked down a tree-lined sidewalk. Bare branches covered with buds still hid tender leaves from the crisp spring air. Evangeline wore her usual school outfit—an oversized sweatshirt, loose Levis, and black Adidas with white stripes. *No sense advertising the fact that I have no curves, right?* Melia, on the other hand, was wearing a jean skirt, tight cashmere sweater that accentuated her 36C's, and black leather knee-high boots.

They passed Evangeline's favorite house—a light-green cottage with pale-blue trim around the windows. The white fence surrounding the cottage was made from wooden slats in all widths and heights that looked like crooked teeth. Evangeline had always assumed an artist lived there because the mailbox was hand-painted. Last year the occupant had depicted Mount Hood, Mount Adams, and Mount Saint

Helens on the dented metal. It was a view only the rich people who lived high in the hills of Portland could afford. A few months ago the scene on the mailbox changed. Now it depicted a dense forest of emerald-green ferns and an aquamarine waterfall cascading onto shiny stones.

Evangeline paused to look at the scene on the mailbox—it seemed three-dimensional and so real she could actually see mist rising from the water tumbling over the edge of the rocks. And she could hear the sound of the rushing water pounding the receiving stones. Evangeline looked up at the sky—blue with fluffy clouds.

"E, what're you looking at?" Melia asked.

"Um…I think I hear rain or something," Evangeline said. She heard it again—a gurgling gush—and looked down. The toe of her sneaker was wet. Water-wet. Evangeline brushed her fingers over the waterfall, wondering if the clear finish the artist had used was dripping, but all she felt was dry paint.

"It's a sunny day! Quit daydreaming—we're gonna miss the bus."

"Sorry."

The girls moved past an old brick clock tower connected to a crumbling rectangular building. The clock chimes began to play a song Evangeline knew she'd heard before, but couldn't quite recall.

"So," Melia teased, "what about Raphe?"

"We're just friends," Evangeline said for the millionth time. Melia had boyfriends on the brain. Evangeline was sixteen and had never been kissed because who'd want to kiss some big-footed giraffe? There were only a few boys in her class tall enough to reach her lips—she was already five-foot-ten and still growing. Her best guy friend, Raphe, always said she'd grow into herself, but she knew he was just being nice.

Raphe's awkward days were long past. He was almost six feet tall with amber-colored eyes framed by dark eyelashes and an olive complexion that flattered his dirty-blonde hair and dimples. Raphe wasn't in any clique or on a sports team, but everyone liked him anyway because he was simply cool. Evangeline had a secret crush on Raphe that she hadn't told Melia about because she knew, without a doubt, that Raphe wouldn't be interested. Plus, there were very few people Evangeline wasn't shy around and Raphe was one of them. *Why make a friendship I cherish awkward by sharing my feelings?*

"Just friends," Evangeline repeated.

"Un-huh." Melia shrugged, flipping her shiny dark-brown hair over one shoulder. Evangeline noticed her friend was toying with the silver bracelet she always wore now, the one with an oversized ruby in its center—probably made of plastic. At the core of the dark-pink stone were thin veins of purple in the shape of a starburst. Melia's boyfriend, Tristin, had given it to her when they'd gone to the spring formal and she never took it off, even though the silver was leaving greenish tarnish marks on her wrist. "Well, I'm totally into Tristin—we're not *just friends*." Melia grinned like the cat that'd swallowed the canary.

"Understandable," Evangeline said, kicking a fallen branch off the sidewalk. Tristin Quin was a transfer kid from the Midwest. He was really good-looking—tall, wavy brown hair, and gorgeous hazel eyes. He hung out with the lacrosse jocks, fascinated with the sport (even though he didn't know how to play), and he was really popular. He'd needed tutoring in math and Melia was a math whiz, so Mrs. Cranmar had asked her to tutor the kid. One thing had led to another. Melia said Tristin told her it was a turn-on that she was so smart. And it was obvious why her best friend liked Tristin. Who wouldn't?

Evangeline was the first to admit that she was more than a little jealous. Melia was super-cute with all the right curves. Boys loved her and although part of that was because she was a huge flirt, most of it was because she was pretty, funny, and smart. Evangeline and Melia had known each other since they were little kids; sometimes Evangeline wondered why Melia had ever stayed her best friend once they got older and Melia became so popular.

"Hey!" Tristin called. Carrying a lacrosse stick one of his buddies had loaned him so he could learn the game, he loped across the street, and casually draped his arm around Melia's waist, hand sliding into her jeans pocket. The trio continued to walk toward the bus that would take them to Jefferson High School.

"It's E's sixteenth birthday," Melia told Tristin.

"Sweet—what'd you get from your folks?"

"It's just me and my mom," Evangeline said. Tristin raised an eyebrow. Evangeline's words began to tumble out before she could stop them because that's what happened when you were bashful and you held all your words in—sometimes they just escaped in a messy, embarrassing jumble: "My mom got pregnant young and the guy split. I never knew him." She finally paused, her cheeks burning.

They reached the bus stop and Tristin flicked stones across the street with the lacrosse stick. "Don't you ever want to try to find your dad?" he asked.

"She asked her mom about him once," Melia said, over sharing, "but she doesn't know where he is."

Evangeline looked away. What Melia didn't know was that her mom had looked so sad that she hadn't had the heart to ask for any details. Her father's name was Richard—that's all she knew or was ever likely to know.

"Dads are overrated," Melia said.

Easy to say when you have one, Evangeline thought. Not only didn't she know her father or his family, but there was no one left living in her mother's line. Her mom's own mother had been a famous prima ballerina named Cleo who'd died in a car accident when her mom was seventeen. It turned out that Cleo had spent much more than she'd ever made and owned none of the extravagant jewels she wore or mansions she lived in. The expensive boarding school Olivia was attending kicked her out when she couldn't pay the tuition. The bank took Cleo's clothes, furs, and cars to pay back some of what she owed them—although they generously allowed Olivia to keep her mom's cat.

All that was left to Evangeline's mom from some distant and long-dead aunt was a small bungalow in Portland, Oregon, so she moved there right after her mother died— alone, and with only $9000.00 and a beat-up guitar to her name. A week later, she discovered that she was pregnant. She tried to contact her boyfriend (the owner of the guitar), but it seemed his dad had been transferred to Europe and the kid hadn't even bothered to tell her he was leaving school or give her an address or telephone number or anything.

It was pure luck that Samantha Harris, a local Portland art dealer, discovered Olivia at a Saturday Market where she was desperately trying to make some money to support herself and her new baby. She'd resorted to painting flowers on glass bottles she'd fished out of recycling bins. Olivia sold them as vases and people lined up to buy them. Samantha saw something unique and marketable in the young woman's work and became her agent, providing Olivia with canvases and quickly selling several small pieces.

Those early sales made it possible for Olivia to have the heat turned on in the bungalow and to buy necessities for the baby. For the next sixteen years Samantha had shepherded Olivia's painting career, turning her into a sought-after artist whose work sold for a lot of money. Sam was also a big sister to Olivia and godmother to Evangeline; they both loved her fiercely.

"So what'd you get?" Melia's question snapped Evangeline back to reality. She unzipped her hoodie to show off the chain and key. Melia's eyes widened. "No way! Your mom never takes that off."

"I know. But she said it's a tradition in our family. Every daughter gets it when she turns sixteen."

Tristin looked up. "Why?"

"She doesn't know, but since we don't have any relatives or other traditions it's important," Evangeline said, then felt idiotic for sounding so serious and added, "to her."

Tristin flicked a stone at a stunning gold and orange butterfly fluttering by and the insect dropped to the pavement by Evangeline's sneaker, one wing torn. "Damn—I didn't mean to hit it," Tristin said, looking at the insect struggling on the concrete.

Evangeline crouched by the butterfly, watching as it tried in vain to fly. Gently she picked it up and smoothed its delicate wing. Not that it would help any, but she needed to do something for the poor thing. Unconsciously, she found herself softly humming a snippet of a song she didn't know the words to, and had never heard aloud, but that often floated through her mind. Suddenly the butterfly flew off.

"Whoa," Tristin muttered. "How'd you do that?"

"Magic," Melia said with a grin, leaning in to give Tristin a kiss that lasted longer than was comfortable for Evangeline.

The bus arrived and they all got on. Raphe had saved Evangeline a seat. "Happy birthday!" He held up a frosted pink cupcake.

Evangeline couldn't help noticing that the morning light brought out the gold flecks in Raphe's brown eyes. He smiled and the dimple in his left cheek winked at her. *He's nice to everyone,* Evangeline reminded herself. *Don't take it personally cause it doesn't mean anything.*

"You look different today," Raphe said.

Evangeline shrugged. "Same old me." But she saw a few of the boys on the bus looking at her and self-consciously tried to smooth her wild curls.

"Quit it," Raphe said, pulling her hand down. "It looks cool—like a lion's mane."

Evangeline took a bite of the cupcake. The frosting came off on her nose and they both laughed.

"What're you gonna do for your birthday?" Raphe's hand still rested on Evangeline's wrist. She knew it was just a co-incidence that he was still touching her, but regardless, she didn't want to move.

"Mom's making lasagna and we'll have carrot cake for dessert. Then we're going to watch "Talladega Nights" for the fifth time." Evangeline rolled her eyes because she knew she sounded pathetic. If she was cool, she'd be having a big party to celebrate her sixteenth; if she was even cooler, someone would've thrown a party for her at a house where the parents were out of town and there was a keg.

"Can I come over?"

"You don't have to do that," Evangeline said. "Not even Melia wants to come over."

"I've only seen that movie seven times. I hear the eighth is the best."

Raphe finally moved his fingers off her wrist and Evangeline felt…disappointed. "Um, yeah, okay. I guess."

On a whim, Evangeline untied her right sneaker, even though she was certain she was imagining things, and pulled out her foot. Her sock was soaking wet.

CHAPTER FIVE

Malledy settled into a chair in the living room of the townhouse he and Juliette had rented in The Pearl District of Portland and opened his book. The letters swam out of focus. He rubbed his eyes, but the words remained slightly blurry. It was a side effect of the higher dose of Paroxetine, but worth it to still the tremors. He closed his eyes for a moment to rest them, thinking back to the past…

. . .

Malledy was ten years old and walking through a stone hallway on the lower level of Castle Aertz. His fingers brushed along the gorgeous silk tapestries lining the walls: hunts with horse and hound and smartly-garbed lords and ladies; the ancient Greek boy, Icarus, flying too close to the sun; various religious scenes including the Last Supper and Madonna and Child; the poet, Dante, his face fearful seeing the ferocious monster who guarded the gates of Hell. Stopping, Malledy stared into Dante's face. "I know how you feel," he told the terrified mortal, because he was afraid, too.

Climbing carved stone steps Malledy passed stunning stained glass windows that filtered the last rays of sunlight and painted the walls amber, ruby, and sapphire. His footfalls were muted as he tread along Persian and Turkish carpets.

"Where am I going?" he asked aloud. But he already knew the answer. He was going to the bonsai garden where his fate would be decided.

Malledy noticed several things when he entered the garden. The ornate bonsai trees were dusted with a light snow. Juliette was standing in the front row of the gathering, her green eyes hopeful, and her breath making tiny puffs of white that evaporated in the cold air. Ninety-three Archivists ranging in age from twenty-eight to ninety-seven were gathered beneath the purple sky that preceded darkness, ready to rule on whether the ten-year-old would become one of them or be removed from the Order.

Otto, the Elder who led the Archivists and Juliette's former lover, nodded to Malledy. A reed-thin man with a perfectly manicured salt-and-pepper goatee, aquiline nose, and deep-set hazel eyes, Otto was known for his brilliance and his unwavering determination to fulfill a client's desires at any cost. He gestured to the gathering. "It's time to make your case, boy."

Malledy walked slowly into the circle of Archivists. Instead of telling them that he was fluent in nine languages, including Clickita, an all but lost African dialect he'd managed to teach himself, or that he could grasp advanced physics, calculus, chemistry, biology and philosophy, he pulled a small, intricately-stitched leather pouch from his pocket.

It had taken Malledy the better part of a year to locate the artifact inside that pouch. After exhaustive research and countless dead-ends, he and Juliette had ended up on a boat through the frigid Pacific Ocean to Easter Island. Once on the island, Malledy had discovered the artifact by following a map chiseled into a flat rock owned by a Mapuche shaman who'd disappeared without a trace. The map had led him to an enormous toppled stone head carved by ancient Polynesians. Inside the head, he'd discovered the leather pouch said in ancient lore to have been a gift from Zeus to his followers.

The discovery should have been reported to the antiquities department of Chile, where it would be catalogued and end up on display in a dusty museum. But that was never going to happen because it now belonged to an Archivist and, ultimately, his paying client. Should anyone have disagreed, Juliette and the other Archivists would have changed their minds—permanently.

Standing among the silent Archivists, Malledy withdrew from the pouch a perfectly smooth, oblong black rock. In its center was a jagged white-marble streak. Mouth dry, uncertain if this talisman would be enough to save his young life, Malledy had held it in his palm and spoken a phrase in ancient Greek. He repeated his words again and again, each time louder, until they began to tumble into each other with force.

The white vein in the rock's center pulsed and started to glow. Malledy looked up to the heavens. Suddenly a fierce lightning bolt ripped the cobalt sky in two. Long after the lightning faded, Malledy's eyes still registered its intensity. Angling the rock in his hand, he boomed the words again. The iridescent silver lightning slashed across the sky like a knife and struck a large bonsai tree twenty yards away from the group, instantly incinerating it. The air filled with the stench of sulfur and burned wood.

"The client," Otto said, taking the rock from Malledy, "will be pleased. What did you learn from this talisman?"

"That rock," Malledy replied, "means there are real forces in the world—different Gods—and a piece of their power can be acquired." What he didn't say was that for a few moments, while he'd been speaking in Greek and felt the rock react to his words and summon a deadly lightning bolt, he'd experienced something he'd never felt before. To the Archivists, he was a mere child—a helpless orphan whose fate rested in their hands. But when Zeus' lightning blazed across the sky, Malledy had been transformed… he'd been mightier than all of them.

"Malledy, do you understand that the acquisition of artifacts is everything? We live to pursue knowledge. We live to acquire talisman. Nothing—no man, no woman, no child, no God—stands in our way."

"Yes, I understand," Malledy said, trying to keep his voice from shaking because Juliette had told him that no matter what happened, he should show no fear.

"Even if I'm removed?" he'd asked his mentor.

Juliette had looked away. "Even then."

Otto looked around the gathering of scholars. None spoke. "Then it is decided. Malledy is one of us."

And so he was. The decision to become an Archivist hadn't been his own, but it was all he had, as there was no family history, parents' footsteps to follow, or other options available. So Malledy relentlessly chased a future devoted solely to research and acquisitions.

When a client decided to pursue seeds from a magical pomegranate, Malledy, by then eleven-years-old with a particular fascination with Greek mythology, was the Archivist for the job. He knew from studying ancient myths that Hades, God of the Underworld, had stolen the lovely Persephone from a meadow while she'd been picking flowers, and raced by chariot down to his dark kingdom with her. Despite Persephone's protests, Hades had forced her to marry him. But there was a twist to the story. If Persephone didn't eat anything in the Underworld, then she'd be permitted to return to earth. Sadly, Persephone did eat some seeds from a pomegranate and once tasted, the seeds made it impossible for her to ever return to earth, ensuring that she would remain Hade's wife for eternity.

Zeus supposedly took pity on Persephone and broke the power of the spell on the pomegranate. This allowed Persephone to leave the Underworld. However, in order to be fair to Hades, Zeus ruled that Persephone had to eat a seed from the magical pomegranate once each year. This act would instantly return her to the Underworld and Hades for a period of six months. When it was time to leave, Persephone had only to eat another seed to return to the living realm.

If there was a legend that the magical pomegranate once existed, Malledy had reasoned, there was a chance it still did. Why a client might want those magical seeds was not Malledy's concern. His sole focus was to track them down and acquire them.

After months of research, travel to distant lands accompanied by Juliette, and frustrating clues that yielded no results, Malledy finally uncovered a diary of a toothless eighty-nine-year-old woman living in Crete that ultimately led him to the treasure. He found the magical seeds in a blue silk sack lying forgotten in the corner of a basement on an olive plantation.

It was Otto, by then suffering from terminal cancer, who withdrew one of the seeds Malledy had obtained and placed it on his tongue. Twenty Archivists witnessed his seven-minute disappearance from bed. When Otto suddenly returned, materializing out of thin air, he was dead. But in his hand was a whole pomegranate and on his face was a smile.

Those seeds were just one of many of Malledy's successes. Over the next five years he pursued and discovered the chain that had been used to bind Prometheus in punishment for stealing fire from the Gods. Soon after, he followed fragments of ancient conversations and cave paintings in Greece to discover the rough reddish fragment of a small trident that Poseidon, God of the Sea, had given to his half-brother, Chiron. The fragment could create massive waves on demand. And one of Malledy's most recent accomplishments was the discovery of a platinum scepter encrusted with enormous rubies and emeralds that had once belonged to Aphrodite, the Goddess of Love and Beauty. Each stone was dazzling and unique, with sapphire, diamond, and amethyst starbursts in their centers.

Of course, all of Malledy's acquisitions were sent to the clients who had paid dearly to acquire them, but the Archivists always retained a tiny fragment of each powerful talisman, storing them in their own vaults. The Archivists had survived through the centuries because they understood that while money was power, ancient artifacts were also power. And Malledy understood this more than most, because the moments when he was allowed to unlock the magic of an artifact and bend it to his will were the only instances in his life where he felt he had an ounce of control....

. . .

A clock in the front hall of the townhouse chimed the hour. Malledy opened his eyes. *What am I now? Who am I now? Do I have any choices left or am I just a victim of Huntington's disease?*

"No," Malledy whispered. "I'm an Archivist and I need to finish what I've begun."

Malledy would find one last artifact for his current client—he was already closing in on success. He'd earn a final and impressive fee for the Archivists and leave Juliette proud of her one-time student and charge. "I'll have come full circle," Malledy murmured. Zeus's lightning stone had been his first discovery. His final acquisition, another of Zeus' creations, would be his last.

"I do have a choice," Malledy's words sounded hollow to his ears. He wondered if his cruel disease would tighten its stranglehold on his body and mind before he found what he was looking for....

Chapter Six

The last class of the day was always the hardest. Evangeline stared out her classroom window at the soccer field where kids in PE were running sprints with varying levels of intensity. Her fingers traced the key at her throat. It felt like it had always been there—like it belonged there.

"Evangeline?" Mrs. Hopkins, stood next to her third-row desk.

"Sorry, what was the question?" Evangeline asked, feeling like she'd been caught stealing. The kids in the English class laughed at her discomfort, but they stopped as soon as Mrs. Hopkins turned to them holding a blackboard eraser. She threw erasers at kids who were passing notes, whispering, or laughing and she had great aim, usually hitting them mid-chest, leaving a rectangular chalk-mark on their clothes.

Mrs. Hopkins turned back to Evangeline, peering at her through oversized horn-rimmed glasses. Her hair was pulled back severely in a low, tight ponytail, and even though she was probably ancient (at least fifty), the English teacher's skin was unlined. "I asked what you thought F. Scott Fitzgerald meant by 'the green light.' So?"

Evangeline felt like she'd been thrust into a spotlight and couldn't find her voice, instead opening and closing her mouth like a fish flopping on dry land. It wasn't that she didn't know the answer—she just couldn't get it out because everyone was staring at her.

"We're talking about The Great Gatsby," Melia hissed from the desk behind Evangeline.

"Zip it, Melia," Mrs. Hopkins warned.

"Fitzgerald used the green light to symbolize Gatsby's hopes and dreams," Lacie offered in an eager voice. "Goth Girl" rarely talked in class, so everyone turned to look at her. Lacie sat hunched in her chair, protected by her dyed black hair, black fingernails, oversized leather jacket, and clunky boots. Too much make-up made her face unnaturally white and the color of her eyes wasn't visible beneath thick black eyeliner and mascara. "What?" she said defensively.

"That's correct, Lacie. Maybe Evangeline can now tell us how the green light is related to Gatsby's fixation on Daisy. Well?"

The bell rang. Thank god.

"Tomorrow there will be a quiz on the various motifs in *The Great Gatsby* including geography, weather, and symbols. I suggest you study for it, Evangeline."

"Want to go to Ben & Jerry's?" Melia asked a few minutes later as they were pulling books from their lockers and stuffing them in their backpacks. "I'll pay."

"I thought you and Tristin were going to hang."

"We can hook up later." Tristin snuck behind Melia and wrapped his arms around her waist, digging his hands into the front pockets of her skirt. He kissed her neck and Melia's eyes closed.

"Get a room," Raphe said as he walked up.

"Sounds like a great idea," Tristin replied with a wink. He glanced over at Evangeline. "E, I can't put my finger on it, but something's different about you today."

"I'm sixteen," Evangeline offered, feeling self-conscious under his scrutiny. All day she'd caught kids glancing at her and then looking away when she turned to them. *Do I look that bad?* Now Melia was staring, too.

"You *do* look different, E. You really do."

"Quit it, you guys!" Evangeline pulled a baseball cap out of her locker, tugging it on to flatten her curls.

"Come on, E, I'll walk you to the bus," Raphe offered.

"What about ice cream?" Melia called out as they walked down the hall.

Evangeline didn't answer because Raphe had draped his arm over her shoulders and she didn't want to do anything to make him take it away. *Not that it means anything.* They walked down the steps outside, passing Lacie, who was sucking face with some guy in a shiny leather jacket who looked old enough to be in college.

On the bus, they talked about World Cup Soccer—loved it; Adele's voice—insane; their dislike of biology and cut flowers—a shame because you were really just killing them; how Ben & Jerry's ice cream was always better than Haagen Daz even when it was just plain vanilla; and why they thought dapper old Gatsby was totally stupid for pursuing the flighty Daisy. When the bus dropped them off at their stop, Raphe walked Evangeline all the way to her house and somewhere along the way, their fingers ended up woven together.

Is this really happening? Evangeline wondered as her pulse raced. *Am I holding Raphe's hand too tight? Too loose? Please don't let my hand start sweating! Raphe is holding my hand. Things like this just don't happen in my world.*

"I'll see you later tonight," Raphe said.

"What for?"

"*Talladega Nights.* Remember? Mind if I come for dinner, too?"

"Course not—your mom out of town again?" Raphe's mom was in pharmaceutical sales and she traveled a ton. His parents were divorced and his dad was out of the picture.

"Yeah—four more days. She wanted me to stay at the neighbors, but the dad smokes and it messes with my asthma."

Raphe still hadn't let go of Evangeline's hand. Suddenly he leaned in and kissed her softly on the lips. After she got over her shock, she kissed him back. *Velvet lips...a hint of wintergreen.* Then it was over and her friend was tossing his skateboard onto the pavement.

"What was that for?" Evangeline blurted out.

"Your birthday."

"So, it was just a one time thing." Evangeline muttered under her breath, but Raphe heard her.

"I sure hope not." He was grinning. "I've liked you for a long time, E, but since you never noticed, I gave myself the deadline of your birthday to do something about it."

"Why?" *Stupid! Don't point out your faults or he'll change his mind!*

"Maybe cause you don't know how great you are."

Evangeline felt her cheeks warm but she didn't mind.

"That okay with you?"

"Yeah." Evangeline was grinning now, too.

"Good." Raphe stepped on his skateboard and she couldn't help but notice how his jeans hung off his hips and the thin band of skin that showed beneath the hem of his shirt. Raphe waved, and rolled away.

Evangeline stood on the porch watching him until he disappeared around the corner. *Sweet sixteen and kissed—Raphe has liked me for a long time?—Can life actually start to be getting good? Sweet sixteen and kissed!*

"Hi, I'm home!" Evangeline kicked the front door closed behind her. She tossed the baseball cap onto the hall bench, kicked off her Adidas, and padded into the kitchen. Usually there was a snack for her on the counter, but today there was only a vase with some flowers that had been wilting when she'd left for school but that now looked freshly cut. Her mom sure had a green thumb.

Jasmine was perched on her favorite window ledge and Evangeline scratched the cat behind one of her drooping ears until she purred. "I'm sixteen and I've been kissed," she whispered to the tabby. Jasmine yawned and closed her eyes. Supposedly the cat had belonged to her grandmother, Cleo, and was at least sixty years old. The vet didn't believe it and neither did Evangeline, but her mom always swore it was true. Regardless, the ancient tabby had probably been kissed a few times in her day and wasn't impressed at all by Evangeline's news.

Her mom wasn't in the kitchen, so she stepped down into the sunroom that doubled as an art studio. An overwhelming, intoxicating perfume greeted her, so thick it was almost palatable. Evangeline wandered into a sea of canvases, some finished and resting on the floor, others sitting on easels half-done or waiting to dry and be transported to whatever gallery was currently showing her mother's work. On every canvas was painted a flower. What made them different from the work of other artists was that these flowers, in vibrant shades and jarring color combinations, didn't exist anywhere in the world—only in her mother's mind. But for some reason they still seemed, well, possible.

A strange notion came to Evangeline. *No, I can't be smelling mom's paintings,* she thought. *They're not real in any sense.* She touched the electric purple flower on a canvas, tracing the hard ridges and swirls of paint. For a heartbeat the petals softened into velvet. Gasping, she snatched her hand away.

There was a canvas set on an easel in the corner of the sunroom that was covered with a paint-splattered drop cloth. It was the painting her mom had been refusing to show her. Evangeline glanced over her shoulder, and then quickly lifted the cloth.

The painting was of Evangeline—or at least of the daughter a mother saw through her own eyes. Using all the vibrant colors she used for her flowers, her mom had fashioned bold brush strokes and sharp edges into a beautiful face. Evangeline stared at the image's eyes. Instead of being too big, they looked feline, slanting slightly upward at the far corners. The blue irises she'd always called eerie were the color of a storm-filled night sky. Her out-of-control blonde curls looked like a lion's mane (like Raphe had said), and her lips, which were still as wide as a jack-o-lantern's, seemed soft and provocative—like they had a secret they were about to share.

"It's me, but it's not me," Evangeline said quietly, absently caressing the black key in just the way her mother had always touched the necklace. Why had her mom made her look like someone she wasn't; someone she was never going to be? The painting felt like a big joke at Evangeline's expense and she ached with humiliation.

Evangeline plucked up a small card resting at the base of the painting and opened it: *To my daughter, Evangeline, who has made my life full of colors I never imagined. I love you, mom.* Instantly she felt ashamed. *I should be thankful that she loves me enough to paint me at all.*

Evangeline raced up the stairs two at a time. "Mom!" she called. "Where are you?" She walked through the upstairs hall, the walls lined with black and white baby photos: Evangeline on a pony; on her mother's shoulders; in Samantha's embrace; at her third birthday; swimming in a pool. "About the painting—I hope you're not planning to hang that monstrosity in a gallery," Evangeline said aloud, trying to keep her tone playful even though she didn't feel all that light and lovely. "If people see your version of me, they'll think you need glasses. Serious, coke-bottle glasses. Mom?"

No answer.

She looked in her bedroom. No mom, just twin beds with green comforters, an antique roll-top desk they'd found at a garage sale, and posters of faraway locales like Bali, Greece and Africa—all places Evangeline hoped to visit when she finally blew out of the fleece-loving, Keene-wearing Pacific Northwest.

She checked the bathroom, hoping she wouldn't find her mom freaking out again. Her mom's weird waking nightmares were really starting to worry her. If it kept happening, she would definitely press her mom into seeing a doctor, which would be kinda hard, since neither of them even had one.

"Where are you?" Evangeline called, opening her mother's bedroom door. She stepped inside and her stomach twisted violently. The mirror had been shattered and bloody glass shards were jumbled on top of the bureau. One white sneaker was poking out from the far side of the bed. She looked away, not wanting to see her mother's thin ankle. But it was too late. Evangeline slowly walked around the side of the bed, heart pounding in her ears, mouth suddenly bone-dry.

"Mom?"

Her mother lay on her stomach. Her right hand was cut along the knuckles and covered in blood. *Did she punch the mirror?* Evangeline knelt down and brushed the hair off her mother's face, fingers resting on the soft skin of her neck. She had a pulse. She wasn't dead.

"Mom?"

Evangeline shook her mother's shoulder. And shook it again, harder. Her mom didn't stir or open her eyes. Evangeline pulled out her cell phone and dialed 9-1-1, gave the operator their address, and told him that her mom was unconscious.

"Is she breathing?"

"Yes, but she won't wake up!" Evangeline's voice sounded like a little kid's. She went back to her mom's side and took her left hand. "Please hurry," she said into the phone.

"Hang in there. You'll hear the ambulance really soon," the operator promised.

Evangeline strained to hear the sirens. But when she finally did, she didn't feel any relief because her mom looked so tiny and broken and she didn't understand how this had happened. It should not have happened! Her mom was really young and healthy. She was also the only family Evangeline had, so she needed to wake up.

"Oh god, please wake up. Mom, can you hear me? Mom? Please—please—please wake up!"

The paramedics put Olivia on a gurney. One of them put an IV line into her hand and hung a bag of clear liquid from a pole at the top of the gurney. "Does your mom do any drugs?"

"What? No! No way!"

"Has she been sick? Cold? Flu? High blood pressure, cancer, kidney, lung or heart problems?"

"No, no, none of that! My mom's super healthy! She's going to be okay. She has to be—she will be! Right? Right?"

The paramedic didn't answer and they rode in the ambulance in silence.

CHAPTER SEVEN

Malledy lay on a couch in the townhouse trying to nap. He'd left early that morning and spent the whole day pretending to be something he wasn't. It was only four in the afternoon but he was exhausted and totally drained. Suddenly Malledy's hand was gripped by a powerful tremor. His time was running out.

There was a knock at the door. "Come in," Malledy called, jamming his hand under his thigh to control the spasms.

Juliette carried in a tray of food and set it on a low table. "How about a snack?"

Malledy looked at the plate of steamed spinach and brown rice—Dr. Aali's prescribed diet. "I'm not hungry."

His mentor sat down in a winged-back chair. "You need your energy."

"Why?"

Juliette tucked her shoulder-length hair behind both ears and met Malledy's gaze. "To fight for your life."

"Who would have thought that a few hand tremors would lead to this?"

"It wasn't just hand tremors, Malledy," Juliette's voice was gentle. "There've been sudden outbursts and misdirected anger. Do you remember?"

Malledy blushed and looked away. "I know. I'm embarrassed. Please tell them I'm sorry."

"You'll get the chance to tell the Archivists yourself."

"I may not live that long and if I do, I won't make any sense." Malledy was supremely aware that very soon he would experience his biggest fear—logic replaced by dementia. *If I was a God, I would never get sick. I would never die. I would be in charge of my life.* "But I'm not a God," Malledy murmured.

"*Quoi?*" Juliette asked.

"Nothing." Malledy shook his head. "Would you mind if I sleep a bit longer? Then I'll eat—promise."

Juliette nodded, kissed his forehead left the room.

Malledy closed his eyes but his mind was churning. Longingly, he thought about the times when he'd felt most in command and powerful, knowing he needed to summon that strength to accomplish his final goal. *I have to do it for Juliette—so she won't be so sad when I'm gone.* His eyes burned with tears.

As Malledy calmed a bit, images shifted in his mind like scattered pieces of a puzzle. First the glimmer of an idea formed—he tried to grasp it, but it slid away. Then he almost had an inspiration, but let it go as if it had burned him because it was too bizarre, too…dangerous. And then, an epiphany struck him like a truck barreling down the highway without brakes—he was simply unable to avoid it. It crashed into him, shattering his defenses, leaving him shaken, breathless.

Malledy opened his eyes and sat up. Throughout his life as an Archivist, whenever he'd held artifacts he'd discovered and demonstrated their ancient magic to his colleagues, he wasn't just a boy or a young man showing off a God's enchantment. His mind, his research, his genius had allowed him to unlock every artifact's power.

In a blinding flash, Malledy made the connection: if he could control elements and individuals with the Gods' ancient artifacts, surely he could control his own destiny with those artifacts. If Malledy had been able to wield the Gods' magic in the past, even as a child fighting for the right to exist within the Order of Archivists, it was not such a great leap to assume that should he find the most powerful talisman in existence—he'd be able to command it, too. If he could do that—and he could—of course he could!—then he could obliterate his disease.

Pandora's Box—the artifact required for Malledy's salvation—was the very artifact he was currently seeking for a client of the Order. Suddenly he realized that fate had conspired in his favor instead of against it.

His cell phone rang and he answered it quickly with the code name he'd chosen for his latest acquisition. "Magnus."

"Cronen," the caller responded with his corresponding code name.

"Were you successful?" Malledy asked.

"No. My two colleagues never returned."

"Don't worry. There are other ways to gain access."

Malledy hung up. Opening his laptop, he typed a security code in Clickita and pulled an image up on the screen. The Google Earth photograph showed a city. He narrowed the parameters to a large neighborhood, then to a single street, and, finally, to a small, solitary pale-yellow house.

"Where *is* it?" Malledy asked the screen, and then, overcome by sudden fury, he slammed the laptop shut. *Stop it.* Shaking with rage, he picked up the laptop, readying to throw it against the wall. *STOP IT!* Malledy forced himself to put the laptop down. *The disease is violent, not me. Not me.* But that wasn't exactly true.

For a moment Malledy felt a profound sense of loss for all that he could've been—should've been. If he hadn't been abandoned as an infant; if he hadn't been forced to become an Archivist or die; if he hadn't been used as a pawn in the Archivists' game of acquisition and mastery over powerful men and governments, who and what would he have become? *I can't change the past so why does it still bother me?*

Shaking his head violently, Malledy forced himself to refocus. He opened the laptop to study the photograph of the yellow bungalow.

CHAPTER EIGHT

Evangeline perched on the windowsill in a stark hospital room that smelled sharply like medicine and bleach. An empty bed with white sheets and a flat pillow jutted from the wall and the blue linoleum tiles were marred with gray wheel-marks. A plump nurse in peach scrubs and a matching headband entered the room, her clogs squeaking. She replaced the IV bag, filled the plastic mug by the bed with water, and then poked a straw into the cup. Evangeline cleared her throat so she didn't scare the nurse.

"Oh, hello, there," the nurse said, only slightly startled. "Who are you?"

"E—Evangeline."

"I'm Stacy."

"Hi. Um, please, can you tell me where my mom is? Her name's Olivia Theopolis."

"She's getting a few more tests and then she'll be brought up here." Moments later a muscular man in green scrubs pushed a narrow bed feet-first into the room. Evangeline's mom looked really pale, with dark purple smudges beneath her eyes, but she was awake.

"Mom!" Evangeline said, leaping off the windowsill. Stacy and the orderly helped her mother slide from the gurney onto the bed while Evangeline hovered at their side. Stacey covered her with a white cotton blanket.

"Are you feeling better?" Her mom nodded.

"I told you that you needed to eat more, Mom! I told her," Evangeline said to Stacy, wincing at the slightly hysterical sound of her voice. "Mom, are you really okay now?"

Before her mother could answer, a group of doctors appeared in the doorway. The man in front had *Dr. Tim Sullivan* stitched on the pocket of his white lab coat. He was about six-foot-three and wore frameless circular glasses. His receding dark-blonde hair was brush-cut and just starting to gray at the temples. Dr. Sullivan stepped into the room and slid a multi-colored scan out of the folder at the foot of the bed. He placed it on the light-board hanging on the wall, his gold wedding band clinking against the board's metal frame.

"Mrs. Theopolis? I'm Dr. Sullivan."

"Hi. This is my daughter, Evangeline," Olivia said.

"Hello," Dr. Sullivan said, reaching out to shake Evangeline's hand. "Mrs. Theopolis—"

"Olivia, please."

"Okay, then, *Olivia*, this is a teaching hospital and residents learn by working with me and discussing each case. Do you mind if they join us?"

"Um, okay."

The residents quickly shuffled into the room, crowding around the light board. They all studied the scan. "Olivia, I think it's best if we discuss this in private."

Olivia shook her head, then grimaced. "Evangeline should be here. I want her here."

"Ah…well, alright then," Dr. Sullivan said. "Who can tell me what they're seeing here?" he asked the residents.

"An abnormal growth in the frontal lobe," a young Asian resident responded. "Malignant tumor."

Evangeline's pulse sped up. She opened her mouth, and then closed it because she didn't know what to say. She'd read somewhere that people in a hospital needed an advocate to look out for them when they were too sick to do it themselves. *But mom isn't that sick, is she?* Evangeline waited for her mom to speak. *Say something, mom. Say something—say something—please.*

"Um, can you tell me, um, how you know it's malignant?" Evangeline finally asked, her voice so soft that the doctors had to step closer to hear her.

"A brain tumor is deemed malignant not just because it consists of cancer cells, but due to its location," the resident answered. "The skull is made of bone and it can't expand to make room for even a small tumor growing in the brain.

With a tumor as large as Ms. Theopolis', it's categorized as malignant due to its location, which can damage and destroy the brain's delicate tissues. Ms. Theopolis complained of severe headaches and vomiting which tell us that she has increased intracranial pressure, or 'IICP.' These symptoms all factor into a diagnosis of malignant tumor."

"Correct, Yuske," Dr. Sullivan said. "What grade are we looking at Veronica?"

Veronica stepped forward, pushing thick, black bangs back so she could more easily peer at the scan. "Looks like a Grade Four."

"What does that mean?" Evangeline asked, embarrassed to hear the tremor in her voice but terribly aware of her mom's silence and the need for both of them to understand what was happening.

Veronica turned to face Evangeline and her mom. "Small tumors with distinct borders are Grade One," she said gently, "which means they are the most easily cured. This tumor is quite large and the borders aren't distinct. Ms. Theopolis'— your mom's symptoms suggest that her tumor is already damaging her brain tissue because she has already experienced headaches, black-outs and delusions."

Evangeline wanted to shout that only crazy people have delusions and her mom wasn't crazy—but hadn't her mom thought her teeth were falling out? And then her hair? What was going on? Evangeline said nothing.

Dr. Sullivan turned to another resident, tapping the scan. "What type of tumor are we looking at, Aaron?"

"Hard to say for certain without a biopsy, but we can narrow the field." The resident scratched his patchy mustache as he thought aloud. "The most common adult brain tumors are metastic tumors, which we can rule out from the MRI scans we've already done, leaving Meningioma or Anaplastic Astrocytoma. My money is on Anaplastic Astrocytoma, and more specifically the sub-group, Glioblastoma Multiforme or 'GBM.'"

"Please, wait! You're going too fast. What's all this stuff you're talking about? What's a GBM?" Evangeline asked the questions, even though she was certain—totally and one-hundred-percent certain—she did not want to hear the answers. What she really wanted to do was to run far away from this hospital and these doctors and their clinical diagnosis of the most important person in her life.

"GBM," Aaron replied, "is a brain tumor made of several different cell types. This makes it difficult to treat because while one type of therapy works on a specific type of cell, another type is needed for each different cell. So we treat GBMs with aggressive chemotherapy and radiation. In Ms. Theopolis' case the tumor is so large and in such an inaccessible area that we won't be able to remove it all without causing severe neurological damage. The best we can do is attempt to keep it from growing and hopefully shrink it a bit to alleviate the headaches and other symptoms."

"The option of surgery shouldn't be entirely ruled out, though," Veronica added, looking to Dr. Sullivan for confirmation.

"It'd create way too much damage," Aaron countered, also looking to Dr. Sullivan.

Evangeline turned to her mother. This roller coaster was climbing way too high and someone needed to stop the ride so they could get off before they started plummeting.

"Mom? Please tell them they're wrong," she begged.

Looking directly into Dr. Sullivan's eyes, Olivia said clearly and loudly, "I'm going to be fine, Evangeline. Could you let me talk to the doctors alone, honey?"

Even though she knew that she should stay, Evangeline nodded, feeling like a coward but unable to stop her feet from trudging out of the room. She slid down the wall and settled on the hall's tiles beside the open door so she could eavesdrop. She swiped at the hot tears running down her cheeks.

"Are you in a lot of pain?" Dr. Sullivan asked.

"Yes."

"Stacy, let's start the IV morphine," Dr. Sullivan said. "You said you've only been symptomatic for a few months?"

"It started with nightmares, headaches, then no appetite, nausea and some vomiting."

"And the delusions?"

"Um…they started about a month ago, but I thought—I guess it doesn't matter what I thought now. I saw things like my teeth and hair falling out, and spiders on my face…"

Spiders? Evangeline clenched her eyes shut and thumped her head against the wall trying to wake up because this had to be another nightmare. But when she opened her eyes, she was still sitting in a hospital corridor beneath harsh, fluorescent lights.

"Hallucinations aren't uncommon with a tumor of this size and location," Dr. Sullivan said.

"I think…it's the same thing that happened to my mother."

"Your mother had a brain tumor?" Veronica asked.

"I don't know, but I heard she had headaches and delusions before her death …maybe it's hereditary?"

"How did your mother die?" Aaron asked.

"She drove her car off a cliff—I was seventeen." She paused. "How long?"

"The tumor is inoperable," Dr. Sullivan said.

"But—" Veronica started.

"It's inoperable," Dr. Sullivan repeated. "We can give you aggressive chemotherapy and radiation and try to keep the tumor from growing, but best-case scenario, you're looking at buying yourself a few months, and in addition to the pain you're already experiencing, you'll have severe nausea, hair loss, and vomiting. Or, we can make you more comfortable. Is there anyone we should call, maybe your husband?"

"No, I'm not married."

"A relative, then?"

"It's just Evangeline and me…and Sa—" Olivia's words trailed off. "Dr. Sullivan," she mumbled, "will you make sure Evangeline gets home safely…dinner, homework—"

Evangeline pulled out her cell phone and dialed a number, listening to the line at the other end ring four times.

"This is Samantha Harris. Please leave a message. Beep."

"Sam, are you there? Pick up—please! It's me. Call me back, please! Call me right away! It's my mom…she's really sick."

CHAPTER NINE

The maze-like greenhouse was jam-packed, filled with rows of tiered plants in all sizes and shapes, creating a forest of rough trunks, swaying stalks, random shocks of bright flowers, and canopies of leaves. Most of the plants were not beautiful. Some were gnarled and yellow-brown, like bunions on an old woman's foot. Others had blossoms that looked like a sickness, weapon, or poison. Vines slithered everywhere—along the floor, climbing the wooden planks, and stretching their greedy fingers up the glass walls. The air was moist, warm, and fetid.

Beeswax candles suspended in battered copper lanterns illuminated the greenhouse. Clad in a long, hooded white robe tied with a belt fashioned from interlocking loops of hammered gold, a woman walked between the narrow rows of plants. Following her was a group of women in matching robes. On the second toe of their right feet, they each wore a gold ring inscribed with a single word: Pandora.

The group entered an open space—concrete floor, glass walls, encroaching brown vines. Candlelight cast vein-like shadows around the room, making it seem like a malignant creature was breathing just beneath the walls. The women formed a circle and began to chant in ancient Greek. The sound washed through the greenhouse like water over time-worn stones, gathering speed, energy, and power until it was a rushing river, fogging windows and making blooms and leaves quiver in resonance.

The leader stepped into the center of the circle and nine of the women dropped to their knees—these were initiates of Pandora who had reached the age to decide whether or not to become full members and pledge their lives to the Sect. One member of Pandora walked before each of those kneeling, pulling back their hoods. As she reached the last young woman, her own hood fell back, revealing Juliette's contemplative face. The remaining followers stepped behind the kneeling sisters' shoulders, bracing them for what was to come. The chanting died away.

The leader took a deep breath, releasing it in a soft sigh. "We are not Gods. We are mere mortals fulfilling the destiny that the Gods have set out before us." She took in all the figures around her, feeling the weight of this moment. "Do you come willingly?" she asked the kneeling women.

"We do," they replied in one voice.

"Will you sacrifice your life for Pandora and her descendants?"

"We will," answered the chorus of voices.

"Pandora is forever," the leader warned. "It is a beautiful and terrible gift."

"Forever," the women agreed. The leader drew a curved blade with an intricate silver handle from the folds of her robe and stepped toward the first kneeling disciple, carving a P deep into her palm. Blood dripped onto the floor. She moved from disciple to disciple until every palm of the kneeling had been branded with a P, the symbol of Pandora, and the concrete was stained red.

CHAPTER TEN

Juliette sat down on the edge of Malledy's bed. "You can't sleep?"

Malledy shook his head. He'd been tossing and turning for hours and Juliette, always in tune with his needs, had brought him a glass of warm milk. "I'm afraid," he admitted to his mentor, taking a sip of the milk.

Regardless of his epiphany from earlier in the day, Malledy knew the sand was quickly draining from his hourglass. He was having more of the violent thoughts and anger Dr. Aali had warned him about and at times he could barely keep himself under control. He understood that Huntington's was trying to worm its way into his brain. When it succeeded, it would be too late to use the artifact he currently sought to excise his disease. He would simply lack the intellectual ability because he would be insane.

Juliette put her hand on Malledy's arm. "You're not going to die. Not if I can help it."

Malledy squeezed his mentor's hand, striving to give her comfort because she didn't deserve to be part of this nightmare. The idea of her becoming his caretaker—feeding him, washing him, wiping his feces when he lost all control, sickened him. He thought about telling Juliette of his epiphany, but chose not to give her what could be false hope should he fail to find Pandora's Box in time. In addition, telling Juliette what he planned would put her in an extremely dangerous position.

Archivists were strictly forbidden to use any artifact they discovered for personal gain. To do so would mean expulsion from the Order. And "expulsion" was the same as "removal." If Malledy told Juliette what he planned and she didn't stop him, then she would be an accomplice. Her life would be forfeit—same as his own. It was better to silently hope for the best but prepare both himself and his mentor for the worst. Malledy took another swallow of the warm milk and steeled himself—it was time to have the conversation he'd been avoiding, dreading.

"Juliette, I know that you wish things were different and that you're trying to make me feel better, but we've always been honest with each other, right?"

Unable to meet Malledy's frank gaze, Juliette stared out the bay window into the darkness. "*Oui.*"

"There's no cure for Huntington's disease—period." Malledy's voice cracked, but he cleared his throat and continued. "I'm most probably going to die a horrible death—paralyzed and demented."

"Malledy—"

"Please let me finish." *If you won't be the grown-up, then I have to be.* "Promise me that if it happens—if I lose my mind—you'll kill me." It felt horrible to ask Juliette to end his life; horrible that he needed to ask; horrible that if he did indeed fail to find the talisman and descended into madness he would have no control and be at his mentor's mercy. *What if she couldn't do it? What if she left him to live like that?*

Juliette was trying not to cry but her shoulders were shaking from suppressed sobs. Malledy gripped her upper arms. "Look at me," he said. Slowly Juliette met his gaze. "Promise me," he demanded, hearing the plaintive note of begging in his voice and hating both of them for it. "Promise!"

Something changed in Juliette's eyes and they lost their softness, instead replaced with a steely resolve Malledy had seen countless times when she was on the trail of an artifact and allowed nothing to stand in her way. "I promise. But it won't come to that."

Malledy felt a wave of frustration crash oI need you to help herg reality. "Modern medicine has no—"

"We don't *need* modern medicine," Juliette interrupted, all trace of emotion drained from her tone. "We need something very much older and infinitely more powerful. But before I tell you a secret I've pledged my life to protect, promise me that what we do next is on *my* terms."

Malledy felt his heart skip a beat. *What secret?* "I promise." And then he hung on every word of Juliette's incredible story. She was a member of Pandora! Malledy knew from his research that Pandora was a deadly Sect created originally by the Goddess Hera.

"The Sect's main function is to protect every descendant of the original Pandora," Juliette continued.

"There's a living descendant?!" Malledy blurted. He could barely control a massive surge of adrenalin coursing through his body.

Juliette hesitated, biting down on her lower lip.

"Please, Juliette!"

"Yes…she's here in Portland. And she might be just the healer you need to survive your disease."

"Why?

Juliette fell silent. "Because," she finally said, "one of the gifts given to the original Pandora was the power to heal. Some of Her descendants have that power, too."

"Please," he said with forced calm, "tell me more." Malledy had hoped to find the Sect because throughout history they had a connection to Pandora's Box. He'd unearthed information about Pandora and knew there was a cell in Portland, but he'd been unable to pinpoint the cell's location, so he'd been focused on locating a secondary talisman that was tied by ancient writings he'd unearthed to Pandora's Box.

How could I have been so blind? In the last few months he had been so engaged trying to locate the other talisman that he'd missed what was right beneath his own nose!

"What's the girl's name," Malledy asked, testing Juliette's commitment to saving him, "and where can we find her?"

Juliette shook her head. Her cheeks burned red and sweat beaded on her upper lip. "I've already said too much. I can't tell you that. I'll go to Pandora and ask for help, but you need to understand that they may not allow the girl to save you."

"Why wouldn't they?"

"She doesn't know who she is. She has no idea of her powers."

"How is that possible?" Malledy was shocked.

"Over the years, her ancestors lost the thread of their own existence. It's easier for Pandora that way. Don't worry, though. I'll ask for their help. There's still a chance for you." She strode to his bedroom door and then turned back to him. "Will you be okay alone for a few hours?"

Malledy nodded, filled with overwhelming gratitude. "Juliette—thank you." His mentor half-smiled and left. He listened to her footsteps echo down the hallway. *I have two chances. And if Pandora won't give me their help willingly, I will take it anyway, because I know much more than Juliette realizes.*

Malledy picked up his cell phone.

"Cronen."

"Magnus. Here's what you need to do—follow Juliette."

Chapter Eleven

"Dr. Sullivan? Please, can I talk to you?" Evangeline was trailing Dr. Sullivan and his residents down the corridor. The group of doctors stopped and turned to face her.

Evangeline struggled to find the right words. "It's just my mom and me," she finally said. "I need her—I need you to help her—*fix* her, not just give her drugs. My mom—Olivia—she's tough even though she doesn't look it. She'd rather be healthy than comfortable."

Dr. Sullivan met her gaze. "Miss Theopolis, sometimes making a patient comfortable is the best we can do, but the course of treatment will be up to your mother. She wanted me to—"

Suddenly Evangeline couldn't breathe, she needed air that didn't smell like medicine—she needed to get outside. She bolted down the hallway toward the elevator. The doors slid open and then closed just as Dr. Sullivan's face appeared in the crack. *Too late.* "This is crazy," she said. "This is crazy!" she screamed inside the empty elevator.

The elevator opened onto the first floor. Evangeline was in the Emergency Room. She walked past some guy with a bloody towel wrapped around his hand and a father holding a coughing, red-faced, infant in his lap. Spying the sliding glass doors, she ran toward them and spilled out into cold, fresh air. It was raining, but the drops felt good on her upturned face. She sank onto a bench, immediately pulling out her cell phone. She tried Samantha again. No answer. She dialed Raphe, but before the phone could ring, she hung up. She thought about Melia. No. She didn't want to say the words. Saying it made the situation too real. Closing her eyes, Evangeline concentrated on counting the raindrops falling on her face.

"Excuse me, Ms. Theopolis?"

Evangeline clenched her eyes. *If I keep them closed long enough this will all be a dream.*

"Ms. Theopolis, is there someone I can call for you? If not, maybe a taxi to get you home?" Dr. Sulliva's voice was kind.

"Um, no thanks. I'll stay here with my mom." She kept her eyes shut.

"Visiting hours ended a few minutes ago."

She finally opened her eyes to look at the doctor. He was drenched, white lab coat and khaki pants dripping onto brown crocs. He'd taken off his glasses and crescents of fatigue underlined his light gray eyes. Evangeline suddenly registered that she was soaked through and really cold. She drew up her knees, wrapping her arms around them.

"You can't stay out here," Dr. Sullivan said. "You're getting cold. Come on."

"Okay." She heard the exhaustion in her voice. "I'll walk home."

The doctor looked at Evangeline with concern. "It's late, dark, and really wet. Your mom asked me to make sure you got home. How about I drive you, alright?"

Evangeline hesitated. *I don't know him. But I don't want to call anyone I know except Sam, and Sam's not home...and he's the only one that can help my mom so maybe I should get to know him.* Finally she nodded, following Dr. Sullivan into the parking lot. They got into a Volvo station wagon that had a babyseat in the back. *Bad guys don't drive Volvos with babyseats, right?*

"What's your address?"

"794 Albermarle. If you take Johnson up the hill for a few miles, then it's a left, third house on the right." Dr. Sullivan cranked the heat and turned on both seat heaters. They rode in silence until they reached Evangeline's pale-yellow bungalow with white trim. Flower boxes filled with red gardenias lined the covered porch.

"Okay, then," Dr. Sullivan said when he'd put the car into park.

Evangeline didn't move. *You have to ask.* "Is she really that sick?"

Dr. Sullivan stared out the rain-splattered windshield. "Yes." Undoing his seatbelt with a click, he got out of the car and walked in the downpour to Evangeline's door, opening it. She climbed out of the car and walked to the front door, the doctor right behind her. When she couldn't get her hands to stop shaking to unlock the door, the doctor did it. He followed her inside and stood dripping on the polished floors. "You mother wanted me to remind you to eat."

"Um, okay—thanks," Evangeline said, certain that there was no way she would be able to swallow even one bite of food. The doctor awkwardly shifted from foot to foot. *Why isn't he leaving?* And then it hit her. *He feels bad about my mom and he wants to say something nice, but he doesn't know what to say to me.* The telephone rang but Evangeline didn't move to get it.

Dr. Sullivan walked over to the old fashioned rotary phone on the front table and picked up the receiver. "Theopolis residence." Evangeline could just barely hear the other voice on the line asking, "Who the hell is this?"

"This is Dr. Tim Sullivan. And you are...I'm sorry, it's hard to hear you—can you turn down the music?"

"I said, Samantha Harris, Olivia Theopolis' agent and Evangeline's god-mother," Sam shouted so loudly that E could hear her. "Is Evangeline there?"

Dr. Sullivan held out the phone to Evangeline and she forced herself to take it. "Hi, Sam. No, it's OK. He's mom's doctor and he's nice…Yeah…I can't hear you that well—" There were bells or something playing in the background—it was a familiar tune…but it didn't really matter, did it? Her mom was in the hospital and she had cancer. Bad cancer.

"Everything's going to be okay, honey," Samantha said. "I promise."

Evangeline felt terror circling her like a shark, deadly and just below the surface. "You can't."

"I promise that we'll deal with this together, okay?"

Deal with this. "Yeah."

"I'll be there soon. Is the doctor leaving now?"

Dr. Sullivan was halfway out the front door. "Um, yeah." Evangeline hung up the phone without saying goodbye. *Do something!*

"Wait! Please—can I show you something?" She walked over to a black and white photograph hanging on the wall at the base of the stairs. In it Evangeline was barely a year old, wearing a pink-flowered bathing suit and floating in the middle of a swimming pool. Her mom was sitting on the edge of the pool, clapping and with a euphoric smile. "I was born knowing how to swim, Dr. Sullivan. My mom was, too."

"Why are you telling me this?"

"People only care about people they know."

Dr. Sullivan walked out the front door. At the last second, he turned and fixed her with an earnest look. "Ms.

74

Theopolis—Evangeline—I'm truly sorry about your mother's illness."

The doctor hustled to the Volvo, shoulders hunched against the rain. Through the doorway, Evangeline watched him drive off. Lost in thought, she traced the onyx key—it felt warmer than her skin and the heat seemed to match the steady pulse of her heartbeat. The warmth started to return to her body in a soft wave and she stopped shivering.

Evangeline closed and locked the front door and walked into the living room, curling up on the overstuffed, shabby-chic couch her mom loved because it was 'just the right amount of worn-in.' Jasmine wandered into the room and climbed onto the couch, nestling beside Evangeline, her head resting against her neck. At some point, Evangeline drifted off into a troubled sleep....

• • •

Riding through the sun-dappled forest atop a thoroughbred whose ebony coat glistened with sweat, Evangeline heard the sound of other horses thundering behind her. She didn't look back lest a low branch sweep her off her mount. The air smelled like the sweet decay of leaves, wet earth, and the musk of dogs and horses. Adjusting her gloved hands on the reins, she gave her mount his head and he moved from a canter to a full gallop.

I don't know how to ride, Evangeline thought, looking down at her attire: a tailored wool coat with black velvet collar and cuffs and tight tan riding britches tucked into tall black leather boots banded with brown. "Where's the fox?" she murmured. Except it wasn't her voice—it was deeper, with a sexy accent she couldn't place and what her mom called a 'bourbon rasp.' Suddenly a red fox darted across the trail. Evangeline dug spurs into her horse's flank and he surged forward. The trees were so thick she didn't see the four-foot-high stone wall until it was only a few feet in front of them. *No!* Her horse leapt, soaring through the air, landing hard on the other side, then lunging onward, up a steep and muddy embankment.

Evangeline's thighs ached as she clung to the horse's back. *Where am I? Who am I?* Her mind scrambled for answers. She knew there was a man named Louis who was her husband and who was much older than she was—they'd married when she was eighteen. Louis liked young women. Now that she was thirty-five, his eyes had begun to stray. *Thirty-five? That's why I have to catch the fox first and prove that I'm still the best horsewoman Louis has ever seen.* Yesterday her husband was flirting with their daughter, Cleo's, young ballerina friends. They were only sixteen. She needed to send Cleo right back to her ballet school in France so that her friends were out of Louis' sight and mind.

Spurring her horse, Evangeline and her mount crested the hill. The red fox darted across a creek twenty yards below. Horse and rider charged down the hill, half galloping, half sliding. Mud splattered Evangeline's neck and face. She could still hear horses behind her and the excited barking of the dogs. She needed to ride faster—she was so close to winning. *I want to get off,* Evangeline thought. *I need to get off this horse!*

They reached the edge of the creek and charged into icy water that pressed around large boulders and flowed with the force of a rain-filled winter and early spring. Suddenly the horse's ears flattened as if he'd heard a call. *Get off!* Evangeline tried to scream, but she had no voice. She kicked her horse again and he lurched forward. Halfway across the creek, the thoroughbred balked and danced sideways, trying to twist back toward the far shore.

"Penelope!" a man shouted. Evangeline glanced toward the bank. A dashing, mustached horseman in a tweed riding jacket, brown britches, and gleaming back boots stood in his stirrups, his expression fearful. "Penelope, come back!" But it was too late.

Evangeline's horse was whinnying, twisting, and bucking. She struggled to stay in the saddle, but her balance was finally broken and she was thrown—airborne, tumbling toward the rocks and water.

"Louis!" she cried. But then her head hit a jagged rock and there was a wet, cracking sound. Color seeped from Evangeline's vision until her world was black and white, flickered once, twice, and then went dark.

• • •

"Louis!" Evangeline screamed. She bolted upright, arms flailing, pain shooting through her head.

"It's okay, honey. I'm here—it's okay—you're okay. Hush." Samantha was wrapping Evangeline in a tight hug.

Evangeline breathed in the freshly-cut-grass scent of Samantha's dark-brown hair. She pulled back and looked at her godmother. Sam's almond-shaped green eyes were red-rimmed. Evangeline had never seen her cry. "Mom's really sick, isn't she?"

Samantha nodded and said, "Visiting hours were over but I *had* to see her."

Evangeline pushed a tangle of curls out of her eyes. "Was she doing okay?"

Samantha looked away. "Olivia thought there were bugs crawling all over her skin. They had to put her in wrist restraints so she wouldn't hurt herself."

Evangeline swallowed the bitter bile surging up her throat. "She can fight the tumor. She can do chemotherapy—the doctors said that'd slow things down."

"Honey, Olivia is—your mom was—she doesn't deserve the humiliation of a slow, painful—"

"But it's *her* choice," Evangeline interrupted. "Dr. Sullivan said it's *her* choice."

Samantha nodded and brushed the side of Evangeline's face.

"What? What's on my face?"

"Just some dried dirt—it's gone now."

And then they just hugged each other because the woman both of them loved was dying.

CHAPTER TWELVE

Juliette eased open the door to Malledy's bedroom. It was nearly midnight and when she'd left him hours earlier, after telling him secrets about Pandora and her descendant, he'd been so agitated she'd been afraid he wouldn't get any rest. She was relieved to see that he was sleeping soundly. Dr. Aali had told her that being rested would help slow the progression of the disease. Any stress would only make things worse. That was why she'd told Malledy's doctor not to tell him everything. If Malledy knew she'd meddled this way, he'd be furious, but she was willing to take the risk because she knew that Malledy couldn't handle the whole truth.

And the whole truth, clearly spelled out in the MRI scans, was that the Huntington's disease had already made Swiss-cheese of the boy's brain. The areas that affect the ability to maintain logic, equilibrium, and control impulses had been severely compromised—eaten away and rotted through. According to the doctor, the disease had been active for some time, possibly as long as two years and well before the irritability and hand tremors betrayed its existence.

It was only because Malledy operated on a much higher mental plane than 99% of the world that he could continue to excel at his work. If the disease were somehow halted now, he might never need to know what the cruel disorder had taken from him. Juliette understood that for a young man who had an intense need to control his life and surroundings, learning what the disease had done already, knowing he couldn't change what it had stolen, would completely crush him.

Tip-toeing to the bed, Juliette rested a hand on Malledy's pale cheek, remembering how she used to comfort him as a child when night terrors would fill his dreams and he'd awake screaming.

"*D'accord*," she murmured, forcing herself to leave the room and return to her own bedchamber to await the phone call that might save Malledy's life.

Malledy opened his eyes as soon as Juliette left his bedroom. He hadn't felt like talking to her. For some reason, he'd experienced a sudden and burning hatred when she touched his cheek. He reminded himself that he loved Juliette and that she had done nothing but try to help him.

Malledy climbed out of his bed and walked over to the narrow window beside his desk, peering out at the rain-soaked sky. For the first time in his life, he was on the verge of complete command of his future. Everything Juliette had told him earlier would lead him to Pandora's Box. In addition, his mentor had identified the descendant. *It's still hard to believe…but it must be true. I should've know—I should've been able to see it without being told.*

A wave of dizziness washed over him and he rested his head against the cool wall until it passed. Pandora's Box was a talisman said in Greek mythology to have been created by Zeus to punish Mankind for accepting fire from Mount Olympus. It was filled with "Furies." The box had been given to Pandora to deliver it to Mankind. But they'd refused to accept the gift. Curious Pandora had opened the box and released the Furies. And the rest was history.

"Or was it?" Malledy asked the empty room with a sly smile. His research on behalf of his client, drawn from long forgotten texts and ancient scrolls, had led him to a different conclusion. And now that truth was going to set Malledy free.

Unbeknownst to the rest of the world, Pandora's Box not only existed, but it wasn't empty. It contained a fifth Fury that the cunning Pandora had managed to trap inside the box: Annihilation. And once Malledy acquired the box and the artifact that was required to open it, he believed that fifth Fury could be manipulated to obliterate his disease.

Malledy picked up the TV remote control and turned on CNN: "A seven-year-old girl in Detroit was found in a dumpster behind her apartment building, beaten, raped—" Malledy changed the channel to Fox: "Hamas has claimed responsibility for a bombing in a popular restaurant in Israel that has killed twenty and left fifteen more men, women and children critically wounded." Malledy turned to NBC: "Iran claims to be well on their way to developing a nuclear weapon."

Disgusted with the brutality and stupidity of mankind, Malledy threw the remote at the TV so hard that it cracked the plasma screen. "If you have absolutely no morals and can't handle freedom," he grumbled at the broken television, "you shouldn't be allowed to govern yourselves!"

Turning to the window, Malledy gripped the wooden sill wishing he could just tilt the world, shake it, and Pandora's Box would slide from its hiding place into his hands. "Patience," he reminded himself. Juliette could lead Malledy to Pandora's Box. And if possessing the box and wielding its power didn't heal him, then he would force the girl to save his life.

Malledy went to his desk and opened his laptop. His screen came to life showing the Google Earth photo of the pale-yellow house. Two figures had been caught in the satellite shot. Their faces were blurred, but both had blonde hair and one was quite tall.

CHAPTER THIRTEEN

Evangeline sank lower in the bath until her hair fanned out in the water and bubbles scented like freesias brushed her chin. The heat felt delicious. She began to sing one of her favorite Italian arias. She was a soprano and her voice was pitch-perfect. The song filled the large bathroom, swelled, dropped, and caressed the white marble. *Italian? I don't even speak Italian.* Evangeline sat up in the bath and looked down at her perfect, size C-cup breasts. *Those aren't mine!* She sank back beneath the water in embarrassment.

"Kiri?" Evangeline's English was inflected with an Italian accent. "The water is cooling. Bring me a towel. Kiri?" *Why do I have a maid if she's never around?* "*Merda.* Stupid girl. I will have Dimitri fire you!" *But then, where would the poor thing go? A towel isn't so important.*

There was a towel beside a radio set on a wide shelf a few feet above the tub. Soft music was coming from the silver box. She reached up to tug the towel free…and the radio came with it, tumbling toward the sudsy water. *Get out!* Evangeline wanted to scream. But the woman just watched the radio spin through the air, holding her breath as the silver box, still playing music, splashed into the water.

Nothing happened. And then a jolt of electricity ran through the woman's feet and arced like lightening, bending her voluptuous, naked body forward, then back, screaming through her legs, pelvis, torso, neck, brain. The woman exhaled one word: "Penelope." She was dead before her body sank beneath the water's surface. And Evangeline couldn't breathe…

• • •

Evangeline awoke abruptly because her hands were clutching at her own neck. She greedily gulped air. *What the hell is going on?*

"What's going on," Evangeline asked aloud, but she was alone in her dark bedroom, the comforter twisted tightly around her body. Sitting up, she felt a rivulet of cold water run down her back. Evangeline touched her hair—it was soaking wet.

How? Maybe she was still caught in the tangled web of her nightmare. But she knew she wasn't. Samantha was asleep in her mom's bed. Tomorrow she'd promised they'd go to the hospital… Her mother was in the hospital.

This isn't fair. This shouldn't be happening. Her clock read 1:23. Evangeline thought about waking Samantha, but decided against it. She'd just say to wait until morning. But Evangeline needed to go to the hospital right now. She had to tell her mom that some really freaking crazy stuff was happening. *She can't die—she can't. She needs to fight her cancer and be there for me. We're a family! One person can't decide to bail because there're only two of us.*

By the glowing light from her clock, Evangeline dressed swiftly and quietly in some jeans and a gray hoodie from the pile of clothes on her floor. On hands and knees, she located one sneaker and searched for the other, feeling along the floor and beneath her bed. Her fingers touched a rectangular box—smooth paper, a stiff ribbon.

Evangeline pulled out the box and held it close to the light of her clock. "For my gorgeous girl. Happy 16th!" was written on the paper in her mother's loose script. Evangeline unwrapped the box, careful not to tear her mom's message. Inside was an iPad. She stared at it for a moment but she felt nothing. She'd wanted the iPad so much only a day ago and now the stupid thing didn't even rate.

Evangeline tossed the gift on the bed, found her other sneaker, eased out her bedroom and snuck down the stairs. Good Samaritan Hospital was about five miles from her house. Grabbing a down sweater, Evangeline slid into the night and started to run.

The streets were soaked. Evangeline didn't feel the rain or the chill in the air. Her mind was racing. Samantha seemed to think her mom shouldn't try to fight or have chemotherapy. But she was wrong. Modern medicine found cures to different diseases all the time. What if they found one for her mom, but they'd all given up too soon? *I want her to fight, even if she loses her hair and barfs her guts out.* In the back of Evangeline's mind she heard a tiny voice saying, 'You're a terrible daughter,' but she ignored it and ran on.

When Evangeline reached the hospital's automatic doors she paused to catch her breath and wipe the rain and sweat from her face. Catching her reflection in the glass, she knew there was nothing she could do about her hair; her curls had grown even wilder from the rain, forming a halo around her face and cascading in a tangle down her back. Taking a deep breath, she stepped through the doors into a brightly lit reception area with modern, leather furniture.

No one will stop me if I look like I know where I'm going. Evangeline made it past the white-haired woman at the admissions desk without a hitch—she'd fallen asleep, head back, snoring. When she pressed the button for the elevator, the door opened instantly. Evangeline stepped inside and pressed six repeatedly until the doors closed. Moments later, she walked out on the oncology floor. The tiles gleamed and the air smelled like bleach, wax and sickness.

Evangeline spied a nurses' station with two women staring at computer screens, their backs to her. She walked down the empty hallway, wincing as her wet sneakers squeaked with each step. No one called out for her to stop. She started to relax a little as she rounded the corner—and ran right into the chest of a doctor in a white lab coat.

"Sorry," Evangeline said, head down, trying to keep walking. The doctor grabbed her arm.

"What're you doing here?"

Evangeline looked up. It was Dr. Sullivan. "Um, I came to see my mom."

"Visiting hours begin at eight in the morning," he said, leading her back the way she'd come.

"Sorry—yeah, okay." Evangeline pretended to follow him for a moment, then pulled free and ran down the hall to her mom's room. She yanked open the door.

At first Evangeline couldn't make sense out of what she was seeing. Ten figures in long, white hooded robes, their faced obscured, were standing in a circle around the bed. They were holding candles and chanting in a language Evangeline had never heard before. One of the figures standing next to her mom's head was holding a pillow over her mom's face! The heart-rate monitor on the wall registered a flat green line and a dull monotone sound was piercing the air. *No!*

"What the hell is going on?!" Dr. Sullivan yelled from behind Evangeline. "Get away from her this instant!"

The figure holding the pillow looked up sharply, her hood slipping back to reveal pale skin, dark brown hair, and emerald-colored eyes. *Samantha?!*

"I did this for Olivia—for your mother," Samantha said. "The Gods are cruel—she deserved better."

And then a sudden freezing wind tore through the room. The candles were extinguished and hell broke loose. There was pushing and shouting and a rush of bodies in the darkness and then a horrible stillness punctuated only by Evangeline's terrified scream and the unremitting sound of her mother's heart monitor emitting that single, flat tone.

CHAPTER FOURTEEN

Someone turned on the lights. The white-robed people in the room had disappeared. Dr. Sullivan yanked the pillow off Evangeline's mother's face and pushed the emergency button above her bed. Moments later, a team of doctors and nurses pushing a crash cart ran into the room. For eleven minutes the doctors and nurses worked to resuscitate their patient using shock paddles, a huge syringe of adrenalin plunged into her chest, and CPR.

Breathing heavily and wiping tears from her face, Evangeline watched it all from her perch on the windowsill, forgotten by everyone, left to be a spectator to her mother's death. But her mother didn't die. The heart rate monitor's green line began to peak sporadically and finally it settled into a rhythm.

"She's okay now," Evangeline said. "She's okay."

Dr. Sullivan turned to her but didn't speak for what felt like forever but was probably only a few seconds. "Your mom is in a coma, Evangeline. The machine you see connected to the tube we put down her throat is a ventilator. It's breathing for her because the part of her brain that controlled involuntary actions, like breathing, was damaged when she was— when she was suffocated by that—that monster."

Evangeline felt her panic rise. "But eventually she'll breathe on her own and wake up? Right?"

Pushing his glasses onto his forehead, Dr. Sullivan pinched the bridge of his nose. "We can't know if there was brain damage, or if the damage was permanent, unless your mother wakes up."

"She *has* to wake up. I need to tell her about Sam."

"Who's Sam?"

The one you just called a monster. "She's my...my godmother—you talked to her on the phone." The doctor looked confused. "Samantha Harris—she's my mom's agent, my godmother. Sam." *Is she a monster?*

"Security can't find those intruders. I'm going to call the police." Dr. Sullivan strode toward the door. "And then I'll phone your godmother to take you home."

Evangeline's hands were balled into tight fists as she struggled to make sense of what she'd seen and to explain it to her mom's doctor. *There's no explanation that makes any sense!*

Wait!" Evangeline called. The doctor turned, looking harried. *Tell him—you can't afford to hide from this.*

"Sam—Samantha—was the woman who—who was holding a pillow over my mom's face!"

"What the hell?!" Dr. Sullivan hollered.

Everything after that was a blur. An athletic-looking, bald detective named Greg Morrison came in asking a million questions. He wanted to know if Olivia was in a cult and if Evangeline was a member, too. When Dr. Sullivan explained that everyone, including Samantha, was wearing hooded robes, Morrison ran a hand over his cleanly shaven face and then continued taking notes. The room was silent except for the scratching of the detective's pencil. When he was done, he read his notes aloud. "So a group of robed individuals, possibly as many at ten, came into this hospital without being seen. One of them—Samantha Harris—attempted to suffocate a terminal patient. When Dr. Sullivan and Evangeline Theopolis—the patient's daughter—entered the room, the lights went out and the entire cult literally disappeared." Detective Morrison looked up. "Do I have the details right?"

Dr. Sullivan, who looked as tired as Evangeline felt, nodded.

"You need to find Samantha Harris," Evangeline whispered. "You need to find Samantha Harris," she repeated loudly enough to make the detective's head snap in her direction.

Morrison scanned his notes. "Samantha—cult member and your legal guardian. Yeah, we've arranged to get a squad car over to her office. You sure that's where she lives, too?"

Evangeline nodded. "Yes. There's a door on the right side of the office that leads to a staircase up to her apartment on the top floor."

"What about Miss Theopolis, detective?" Dr. Sullivan asked. "Shouldn't you provide some kind of protection for her?"

"If they'd wanted to hurt her, they would've tried to kill her instead of her mother."

Dr. Sullivan frowned. "How can you be so sure?"

"I'm as sure as I can be, doc, with an understaffed police department that's currently waging a war on meth, gangs, and prostitution. From the sound of the situation, Samantha Harris had plenty of opportunities to off the kid at home, and murder, unless it's fueled by rage, is usually a crime of opportunity. My bet is that Miss Theopolis isn't in danger right now, but we can't leave her home alone so we'll drop her off at juvie tonight."

"Juvie?" Dr. Sullivan gasped.

Morrison walked toward the door. "She's got no other family and her guardian isn't gonna take her in since if we find her she's going to jail. Anyway, it's too late to get her in a group home. Tomorrow her case will be turned over to Social Services and if she's got no other family, she'll be placed into our country's foster care system."

They're talking about me like I'm not even here! Like I'm invisible! Evangeline thought about calling Melia. Surely her step-mom would let her stay at their house. But then Evangeline would have to explain everything to them. *My mom has cancer—it's in her brain—it's terminal—Oh, and Samantha tried to kill her tonight.* Evangeline would rather risk it in juvie than say those words aloud, because if she said them to Melia, the entire situation would be public because her best friend had a big mouth.

"She can stay at my house for the night," Dr. Sullivan said quickly.

"What?" Evangeline and Morrison asked in unison.

"Why would you do that, doc?" Morrison asked, echoing the very question in Evangeline's mind.

"Because I don't think a girl who's just witnessed her mother's attempted murder should spend the night locked up with a bunch of thugs and criminals. I'll bring her to the police station first thing in the morning. That work?"

Detective Morrison eyed Dr. Sullivan for a long moment. "I'll make a call. Give me a minute."

A few minutes later Morrison returned. "Yeah, doc, that works. You bring her down first thing tomorrow morning." He made to leave and said over her shoulder. "Don't either of you leave town."

CHAPTER FIFTEEN

It was seven o'clock but Juliette didn't wake Malledy. She settled in a chair by his bed and watched him sleep as she'd done so many times when he was a baby. His brow was furrowed and she noticed that the tremors were creeping up his arms. The disease was progressing, swallowing body parts of its victim with relentless determination. Malledy mumbled in his sleep and Juliette made sense of a few of his words.

"Lightening bolt...*fille*...Portland...ahhh... *la clé*... mmmhph..."

Juliette leaned forward. *Fille* was French for daughter. *La clé* meant key. *Could it be coincidence? Could it be nothing more than the ramblings of a sick young man?* Juliette felt a tingling of foreboding.

"*Non,* it's impossible." *I'm so tired, so heartsick, so frustrated, that I'm overacting.* But the fear inside her refused to stop growing. *Have I made a terrible mistake?*

Juliette had not told Malledy names or locations when discussing Pandora or the descendant. *But what if he's known all along?* He had chosen his own physician who was located in Portland—was that a coincidence, too? Maybe…but how could Juliette ignore the fact that Malledy had said *daughter* and *key* in his sleep?

Malledy was still a brilliant young man. He was fighting for his life. If anyone could find out the truth, despite thousands of years of the Sect creating fictitious documents, misdirection on the highest levels, obfuscations, and false mythology (and when all else failed, countless murders), it would be him. Either way, Juliette needed to find out; she had a responsibility to find out. A wave of horrendous guilt washed over her. *Have I told Malledy too much? Have I ignored who he's become?*

Juliette sat down at Malledy's desk and opened his laptop. She felt another pang of guilt and glanced at her right palm: the P forever scarred into her skin so long ago was faded. *They must be my first allegiance.* She closed her eyes.

Juliette was not a young woman anymore and leading a double life had taken its toll. A member of Pandora since she was a teenager, she'd joined the Archivists at twenty-three, sought out by the Order for her ground breaking work in several long-forgotten and seemingly dead Asian dialects.

Her research had been specifically designed by Pandora to interest the Order because the Sect wanted one of their members to be firmly embedded in the Archivists' powerful organization. If, the Sect believed, anyone were to find out Pandora's secrets, it would be the Archivists, so it was important that a woman lived within Castle Aertz to monitor the other Archivists' work.

Juliette had never wavered in her loyalties. She belonged to Pandora and the Sect was far older than the Archivists and far more deadly. As a member of Pandora, Juliette could not think twice about protecting all they stood for. About protecting the descendant. Even now, as she asked Pandora to allow her to save Malledy's life, she knew that she might be called upon to sacrifice him.

Why did I tell him all I did? "Because he'd lost all hope," she whispered and opened her eyes. She began trying passwords and wasn't surprised to see her attempts to break into the laptop fail. Malledy was a genius. If he had accomplished the unthinkable—finding Pandora and the descendant as well as both talismans, he had done what only a score of men and women had accomplished over thousands of years and none of them lived to tell the tale.

Malledy moaned in his sleep and Juliette turned to look at him. *Have I put everything I have pledged my entire life to protect at risk? And if what I fear is true, will I tell the leader and sacrifice you? Do I have a choice?*

Malledy began to make a strange clicking sound with his tongue. Juliette pulled out her iPhone and pressed the "record" button. "Clkkk-tkkk-phtkkk-o-kkkl-dmgkk-clkkk-b-tkick-vokk-nkkkk..." Malledy's tongue clicked rapidly against his palate. When he fell silent, Juliette pressed the "stop" button on her phone and stood. She needed to have the Archivists' Director of Languages download a file from the audio lab to her computer.

The Archivists' audio lab contained every language and dialect known to the world and even some thought lost. If Juliette was right, Malledy was speaking in Clickita. He was probably the only outsider in the world fluent in that African dialect, which had fascinated him as a child. Now, as his brain was deteriorating he was reverting to languages he'd taught himself in his youth.

Perhaps, Juliette thought, *I can learn more from his nocturnal ramblings before I jump to a conclusion.* No one could fault her for being certain, could they? To bring her suspicions to Pandora and not only end her hopes for their help, but sign Malledy's death warrant would not only be premature but unconscionable. *I must be certain,* Juliette thought, closing Malledy's laptop quietly and walking toward the door. She almost felt righteous about her decision.

CHAPTER SIXTEEN

Evangeline recognized the mirror. It was the antique with hazy glass that hung over her mother's bureau. She stood in front of it and her reflection stared back at her: blonde curls around a heart-shaped face. Strange, she'd always thought her face was oval and way too narrow. Her dark-blue eyes curved slightly up at the outer edges, just like they had in her mom's painting, appearing feline and strangely predatory. For the very first time, Evangeline noticed tiny gold flecks in her irises. Her tongue darted out, licking her lower lip in a nervous habit she hadn't known she'd acquired. "This isn't me." Her lips were still too full, but somehow they'd found a balance within the rest of her features and beneath a nose she'd always considered far too wide. Even her long neck seemed different—almost graceful instead of giraffe-like.

"This isn't me," Evangeline repeated. And then a red-hot poker dug into her temple. She winced, fingers flying up to press against her left eye. Evangeline gripped the edge of the bureau to keep from falling. The pain swelled, burrowing into the smallest corners of her mind with sharp claws. Evangeline's vision narrowed, swirls and stars sparkling in front of her eyes, she opened her mouth to scream, and then, just as suddenly as it began, the agony receded, leaving her sweating and short of breath.

"What the hell?" Evangeline opened her eyes and looked at her reflection. But it was her mother's face staring back at her.

"Help me, E," her mother was begging.

"Mom! Tell me how!"

Her mother's reflection pressed the tips of her own fingers into her left temple, the blue vein pulsing. The vein grew larger and bulged between her mother's fingers, taking on a bumpy consistency, as if there was something other than blood pumping through its walls. Abruptly, her mother's temple tore open and hundreds of tiny black spiders burst out in a stream of cherry blood! Evangeline gasped. The spiders skittered across her mother's face—a sea of hairy-bristled, yellow-eyed arachnids—and streamed into her nose and mouth. As her mother's eyes rolled back until only the whites showed, Evangeline punched her fist into the glass…

. . .

Evangeline woke in a burst of pain. The knuckles of her right hand were scraped and bleeding. She licked away the blood. *Another nightmare. But was it?* She couldn't stop herself from wondering if what she'd just dreamed had really happened to her mom. *She asked for my help. How can I help her now?*

Evangeline looked around. *Where am I?* The room she was in was pastel-green with yellow bears stenciled along the baseboards. There was a white crib in one corner, and above it were two small paintings of iridescent purple flowers so shiny, it seemed the blossoms were three-dimensional. Evangeline recalled her mom painting those flowers a few years ago. On the far wall, beneath a large picture window, was a bureau that matched the crib. The knobs on the drawers depicted Winnie the Pooh, Owl, Rabbit, and Tigger.

Evangeline hadn't seen any of this at four o'clock when she'd finally fallen onto a futon couch, pulled a blanket over her, and instantly passed out. She rolled off the futon, made a weak attempt to smooth down the clothes she'd slept in, and walked over to the paintings, stopping when she smelled their intoxicating scent. "They're not real," she said, and instantly the perfume was gone.

A man cleared his throat and Evangeline turned to see Dr. Sullivan standing in the doorway of his kid's nursery. "Um, hi," she said, looking at her feet because she suddenly felt overwhelmingly awkward and self-conscious. "You didn't tell my mom you owned some of her paintings."

"It wasn't pertinent." Dr. Sullivan was already showered and dressed for work—a starched white button-down shirt, khakis, and brown leather shoes. *He could be in a Timberland catalogue*, Evangeline thought as she peered at him. "There's some cereal and milk in the kitchen."

"That's okay—but thank you. I'll just eat something later at the hospital."

Confusion colored Dr. Sullivan's expression.

"What's wrong?" Evangeline asked, quickly looking down to make sure her shirt was on straight and the fly of her jeans zipped.

"It's just—you look different."

Evangeline shrugged, trying to flatten her hair. *Maybe I look different because I watched my godmother try to murder my mom last night—that'll change a girl quick.*

"It all really happened, didn't it?" She forced her eyes to meet the doctor's.

"I'm sorry—yes. Detective Morrison called. Samantha Harris' office and apartment were totally cleaned out. Morrison said whoever did it was a professional and didn't leave a fingerprint or anything else that could identify Sam. And there's no Social Security number for any Samantha Harris. So, according to Morrison, your godmother has vanished without a trace. I'm so sorry." Dr. Sullivan walked back into the hall. "Morrison said to bring you by the station so he can fill out paperwork and someone can take you to a group home."

Group home? What does that mean? "Will I still get to see my mom?"

Dr. Sullivan ran a hand through his short hair. "I really don't know."

Don't panic—don't panic—think. "You have to go to the hospital every day, right?"

"Yes, of course."

"Then can I—can I please stay with you a little bit longer, just so I can spend time with my mom?"

Dr. Sullivan shook his head. "Sorry, but no can do. You really should eat before I take you to the police station."

Evangeline pushed cold cereal around a blue ceramic bowl in the kitchen of Dr. Sullivan's modern house. She noticed that there was a large pile of unopened mail on the counter and a lot of gift-wrapped boxes and pink gift bags on the floor. Dirty dishes filled the sink. Pictures of who Evangeline quickly surmised was Dr. Sullivan's gorgeous wife were stuck with magnets on the sub-zero refrigerator. In one, the woman was in Middlebury sweatshirt riding a bike, her brown ponytail flying. In another, the couple was grinning on a red-plaid picnic blanket. A third shot showed their wedding day. They looked like the couple on top of a five-tier cake. There was also a black and white sonogram on the fridge door.

"So, are they on a trip?"

Dr. Sullivan's pager went off and he pulled out his cell phone to dial a number. "Dr. Sullivan…Yes…Okay, I'll be there in fifteen." He hung up and looked at Evangeline.

No more bad news, Evangeline prayed. *No more.*

"One of your mother's kidneys has stopped functioning. The other is working at thirty percent."

Evangeline's fingers darted to the key. The smooth stone gave off tiny prickles of electricity. She had the strange notion that maybe the feeling was her mom reaching out—but that was crazy. *Quit it! Crazy is the last thing you need right now.*

"Dr. Sullivan, can you explain to me what the kidney thing means?"

"The part of your mom's brain that regulated her kidneys isn't working anymore. We'll monitor her still-functioning organ and put her on dialysis if necessary. But—"

"But, what?" *Why do I keep asking questions when I don't want to know the answers?*

"I'm sorry—but when this happens to the kidneys, it's the first step in her body breaking down."

"Let me go with you to the hospital!" Evangeline begged. "Please!" A shiver ran down her spine and she recalled the childish idea that a chill meant someone had just walked over the grave of a person you loved. "Please! I need—I deserve the chance to say goodbye, don't I?"

Dr. Sullivan hesitated, then grabbed his keys and headed to the door. "Okay. Let's go."

They rode in silence for a while.

"Why did you help me last night?" Evangeline finally asked.

"Because no one should be all alone at a time like this—especially not a kid." Dr. Sullivan reached below his seat and pulled out a silver thermos. He put it between his knees and unscrewed the top, took a swallow and then screwed the cap back on.

"We can swing by Coffee People and get you fresh joe," Evangeline offered, figuring the stuff he was drinking would have to be pretty nasty from being in his car for who knows how long.

"I'm fine."

Evangeline nodded, but she had the distinct impression that Dr. Sullivan was lying.

CHAPTER SEVENTEEN

Juliette watched Malledy put books and folders in his black backpack—the backpack he'd insisted on buying to attend classes that were so remedial for him as to be ridiculous.

"I want to experience what it would've been like to be a normal kid," Malledy had said, "while there's still time."

I believed him, Juliette silently thought, *because I wanted to believe. Just as I wanted to believe that his choice of a physician practicing in Portland, Oregon was a coincidence.* She had left Castle Aertz and flown with Malledy to Portland seven weeks ago so that Malledy could be poked, prodded, imaged, and treated like a guinea pig by Dr. Aali, the specialist he'd said might be able to find a cure, or at least give him more time.

And Juliette had let Malledy attend a local high school, even though he had to take a triple dose of anti-spasmodic drugs so his tremors wouldn't be visible to the other kids. All because he'd wanted to be live out a fantasy of what life would've been like if he hadn't been brought to the castle; if he hadn't been a genius accepted into the Order.

"You look exhausted," Malledy said, hoisting his backpack over one shoulder. He wore the New York sweatshirt he'd insisted on buying when their plane had landed at JFK airport, jeans that hung off his hips, and Nikes.

"I didn't sleep much last night."

"Maybe you should take a rest—"

"I know."

Malledy looked at her quizzically. "Juliette, are you okay?"

"Last night I translated words you mumbled in your sleep. You were speaking Clickita."

Malledy's raised his eyebrows. "I was? Okay, but why would you do that?"

"Don't you want to know what you said?"

Malledy walked over to the window by his desk and stared out at Mount Hood. "It's not much of a mountain compared to the Italian Alps, is it?" He turned back to Juliette. "Say what you want to say."

"I couldn't translate all of it, but I got enough. Mother. Key. Daughter. Box. Need both."

"What does that mean?" Malledy asked, appearing confused.

Juliette wasn't buying his act. She was not a genius, but she, too, was brilliant. "That you know that there are two descendants; that you know that there are also two artifacts; that you are trying to acquire both of those talismans!"

Malledy shrugged and sat down on the bed. "Isn't that what we do, Juliette? We're Archivists. We acquire, through any means necessary, talisman for our clients. *You* taught me that."

Juliette felt her blood run cold. "Why would you hide your work from me?"

"I wanted to surprise you," Malledy said earnestly. "To make one final acquisition for you to be proud of before I lost the ability to walk, let alone talk and think."

Juliette's heart felt like it was literally being torn in two. "Malledy, don't you understand that I was placed into the Archivists' Order by Pandora to guard against this instance?"

Malledy stared at the carpet, unable to meet Juliette's gaze. "But I'm dying."

"You are playing a deadly game." *You are losing your mind.* Juliette sat down next to Malledy and took his hand. "So much can go wrong, mon fils."

"Listen to me," Malledy said, squeezing her hand. "I don't want the artifacts."

"Liar."

Malledy looked truly wounded. "In another life, maybe, but I just want to live. At first I was just looking for Pandora's Box for a client—I swear. Finding the key was a means to that end. But then you told me about the descendant and her ability to heal me. You gave me hints—you practically led me to the Sect!"

Juliette felt like she'd been punched in the gut. For a moment she couldn't breathe and an intense wave of nausea washed over her. *He's right. I've betrayed Pandora. How can I make this right?!*

Malledy rushed on. "Listen, Juliette, please! You've said yourself that the chance that Pandora will allow the girl to heal me isn't a given. So I need to have a fall-back plan. If I have the artifacts, the Sect will have to make the descendant heal me! Once I'm better I'll give both talismans back. I swear it! And I'll tell the client that I hit a dead end and couldn't find the box. Don't you see, using the box and key as leverage are my only hope!" Malledy began to cry. Embarrassed, he turned away.

"Don't," Juliette said, putting a hand on his shoulder.

Malledy grabbed her wrist, his grip tight as a vice. "Then tell me where Pandora's Box is hidden—your Sect must know!"

"You're hurting me," Juliette said, wincing.

Malledy immediately let go. "I would never hurt you. Never. But time is running out for me. Every day it's harder to make my muscles respond. Soon the disease will attack my brain and if I haven't located the box, then there's no hope for me."

"What about the key?" Juliette demanded. Malledy met her gaze. *He knows where it is.* "I don't know where the box is," she admitted. "I've never had the need to know." This was the truth and she could see that Malledy believed her by the crestfallen look on his face.

"But your Sect has it?"

Juliette looked away and that was answer enough.

"Juliette, you have to find Pandora's Box for me," Malledy begged. "It may be my only chance!"

He can no longer be trusted. Juliette took a deep breath and then exhaled. "I will try to find the box for you," she said. Malledy wiped his runny nose with the back of his hand, just as he used to do as a little boy. Her heart ached. *He's no longer that boy...but is he now my enemy? Is there a way to help him without hurting the descendant and my Sect? Can I take the risk of watching and waiting to find out?*

"You would do that...for me?"

"Go to school. I'll do what I can."

Malledy hugged Juliette so tightly that for a moment she couldn't breathe. Then he walked toward the door, his back to her, and she pulled a snub-nosed silver revolver out of her pocket.

CHAPTER EIGHTEEN

Evangeline's mom looked really, really awful. There was a tube taped to her cheek and lodged in her mouth, going down her throat. Her skin was horribly white and her normally shiny hair was flat and dull. The ventilator, an ugly black accordion in a clear capsule, pumped rhythmically, reminding Evangeline with each beep of the heart monitor that her mom was still not breathing on her own.

I've got to do something to help my mom now, because once I'm in a group home, I may not get the chance to see her again. Evangeline gathered her courage and turned to face Stacy, who was changing the IV drip.

"What if—what if I want a different doctor for my mom?" she asked. Stacey didn't look up. *Stop being timid and try again.* "It's just that I don't think Dr. Sullivan wants my mother to do chemo or fight her disease or anything, and

I need a doctor who believes my mom has a chance, you know?"

Stacy stopped what she was doing and fixed Evangeline with a steady gaze that made her feel about two-inches tall. She pushed on because she was the only advocate her mom had left.

"I listened to the residents talking and Dr. Sullivan is all about painkillers. He won't even consider doing surgery to get rid of my mom's tumor."

Evangeline reached for her mom's hand. The fingers were beginning to curl inward—like claws. She felt a sense of overwhelming dread that made it hard to breathe, but she continued. "I'm not—I'm not saying Dr. Sullivan is a bad doctor—I'm sure he's not—and he's been nice to me, so I definitely don't want to get him in any trouble. But I need to help my mom get well any way I can."

Stacy shut the door and turned to face Evangeline. "Listen, Dr. Sullivan is the best, bar none, oncologist in this hospital. People come from all over the world so he can treat them. And he saves a lot of lives, or at least prolongs them so fathers can see their kids grow up; mothers can watch their daughters get married; and teenagers can learn to drive and go to their proms. I know. I've seen him practically work miracles. Dr. Sullivan would do *anything* to save your mom if he could."

Evangeline's frustration overflowed. "That's not true! He's *got* a real family. He can't possibly understand how important my mom is to me—that it's just the two of us. There's no way he can get what we're going through."

Stacy stared at Evangeline like horns were suddenly growing out of her head—like she was some kind of monster. "You don't know. Of course you don't. How could you?"

"Know what?" Evangeline demanded in a fervent voice she'd never heard herself use before.

"Don't be so quick to judge, okay? Only two weeks ago, Dr. Sullivan woke up to find that his wife had died sometime during the night from a pulmonary embolism. She was eight months pregnant."

"Oh my god." Evangeline winced and gripped her mom's hand tightly. "The baby?" *All those unopened pink gift bags.*

"The baby died, too." Stacy sat down at the foot of the bed. "Look, Evangeline, I'm sorry—really sorry. This situation, well, it sucks for you, I get that. But changing doctors isn't going to alter what's happening to your mom. And Dr. Sullivan is the best. He knows what's at stake."

Walking to the window, Evangeline stared out on the gloomy gray morning. "I feel like it's all my fault," she said softly.

"What is?"

"I haven't been the greatest daughter. I knew something was wrong with my mom—all these weird symptoms—and I ignored it—because it scared me. And the day I found my mom unconscious in her bedroom...she'd made me a painting and I called it a monstrosity. I pretended I was kidding, but I wasn't."

"Was it?"

Evangeline half-laughed, half-sobbed. "Nothing my mom ever painted was a monstrosity. It was beautiful—but it felt like a slap in the face."

"You have something in common with Dr. Sullivan," Stacy said.

Evangeline shook her head. "I have nothing in common with him."

"He thinks his wife's and daughter's deaths were his fault, too."

"Oh no. Were they?"

"Embolisms are like cancer. They just happen."

"E," a girl's voice called out. Evangeline turned and saw her best friend pushing open the door. Melia had dressed hastily—no makeup, unbrushed hair, torn jeans, sneakers and an oversized sweater.

"Melia! What are you doing here? Evangeline said. "You look awful."

"Thanks a lot. You…don't." Melia came into the room and wrapped Evangeline in a tight hug. Evangeline didn't move, willing to let Melia try to hold her together.

"She's really sick, M."

"I know. I'm so sorry."

Evangeline breathed in the familiar cinnamon scent of her friend and for just a second tried to pretend they were somewhere else—but it didn't work. When she opened her eyes, she saw Tristin in the hallway, shifting uncomfortably from foot to foot and nervously spinning that lacrosse stick. He looked awful, too, like he'd had about as much sleep as she'd had the last few nights.

Stacy gave Evangeline's arm a squeeze as she headed out the door. "Trust Dr. Sullivan, okay?"

"Yeah, okay, and thanks," Evangeline said.

Raphe walked up beside Tristin and raised one hand in a shy greeting. "Hey, E."

"Hey. Oh, I'm so glad you're all here. But…how'd you guys find out?"

"Bad news travels fast," Melia said. "Samantha's murder attempt on your mom was front page of the Oregonian. Why didn't you tell us?"

"How'd you get out of school?"

"Duh, we're skipping. This is way more important than school." Melia grasped Evangeline's hands. "Why didn't you call? My mom would've picked you up last night. You could've stayed with me."

Evangeline shrugged. "I know. I'm sorry. I just couldn't say the words, you know? It would've made everything too real. And Samantha…I thought she loved us." And then Evangeline was crouching on the floor, sobbing hard with Melia and Raphe's arms around her, trying to keep her from shattering into a million pieces.

"There's a manhunt out for Samantha Harris," Tristin offered from the doorway.

"I don't think they'll find her," Evangeline said when she finally stopped sobbing. "The detective on the case said she's disappeared without a trace. Sam didn't have a Social Security number and I bet we never even knew her real name. Can you believe that? I don't even know my godmother's real name?!"

"Hey gang, I don't think your friend has had breakfast," Stacy said, popping her head in the room. "Why don't you head down to the cafeteria and get her something?"

Evangeline stood up, wiping her face on her sleeve. "I'm not really hungry. Besides, I don't want to leave mom."

"I'll page you if there's any change. I promise, kiddo."

Evangeline went over to the bed and kissed her mother's pale, dry cheek, then allowed her friends to lead her into the corridor. They passed Dr. Sullivan and his passel of residents. "You guys go ahead," Evangeline said. "I'll meet you down there. I need to talk with the doctor a sec." Her friends didn't budge.

"I'll wait with Evangeline," Raphe offered. "Okay, E?" Evangeline nodded. "I'll bring her to the cafeteria after she's done." Melia hesitated and then she and Tristin headed for the elevator.

"Looks like your friends are here," Dr. Sullivan said. "That's good."

"Yeah. Um, can I talk to you alone?"

"Sure." Dr. Sullivan led them down the hallway, out of hearing of Raphe and his residents.

"Your family—" she began. She so badly wanted to find the right words, but was unable to articulate that she didn't believe their deaths had been his fault, that she knew no matter what, nothing would make that raw feeling go away. "Thanks for giving me the chance—to say goodbye to my mom."

Dr. Sullivan held Evangeline's gaze for a long moment and then adjusted his lab coat and walked away to join his residents.

"What was that all about?" Raphe asked, holding her hand.

"Turns out Dr. Sullivan and I have something in common." Evangeline twined her fingers through Raphe's; it made her feel a little bit stronger. "Thanks so much for coming."

"Of course, E. What a crummy birthday." Raphe paused. "You know, my mom's still out of town. You can stay at our house if you want."

Butterflies fluttered in her stomach. Had it only been yesterday that she'd had her first kiss? They passed a patient lounge—lots of sickly looking people attached to IV drips filling them with fluids, chemo drugs, and pain killers. They looked like the walking dead. *Do I really want that for my mom?*

The television in the lounge was playing an old Julie Andrews movie—"The Sound of Music." Evangeline had seen it a million times because her mom loved corny movies. Captain Von Trapp was singing Edelweiss. "Soft and white, clean and bright, bless my homeland forever." Something about the song made Evangeline stop. It wasn't the words. No, it was the tune. "Blossom of snow may you bloom and grow—" She'd heard that song recently…where?

"Evangeline, everything is going to be okay. I promise…" Samantha had said when she'd called to say she was on her way to take care of her. There'd been bells ringing in the background. But it hadn't been bells. It had been chimes from "Edelweiss." The same chimes Evangeline sometimes heard…Where had she heard them recently?

"Evangeline?"

Oh! In the clock tower of the crumbling old building she passed every day on her way to the bus stop.

"Raphe, I know where she is!" Evangeline exclaimed.

"What? Who?"

"Samantha Harris."

"Well, we should call the police!"

"No!" *What am I saying? Why not?*

"Come on! She tried to kill your mom. She deserves to go to jail."

"I agree. But—but I want to see her first. I need to know why. Once I hear the truth—from Sam herself—then we can call the cops." Evangeline rushed toward the closest exit stairway.

"But what if she's dangerous?"

"Detective Morrison said if Sam had wanted to kill me she'd had plenty of chances already."

"Well, how are you so sure? I'm going with you!" Raphe followed Evangeline into the stairwell.

"I was hoping you would," Evangeline called, leaping down the steps three at a time and ignoring the jangle of her nerves and the voice inside her head screaming for her to stop before it was too late.

Chapter Nineteen

The city bus rounded the corner, slowed, and squealed to a stop. Evangeline and Raphe rushed down the aisle and out onto 25th Street. The sky was slate-gray and it had begun to pour again, the sidewalk more a moving stream than concrete. They ran, their sneakers soaking through as they splashed through deep puddles. Evangeline felt the rain saturate her down sweater and hoodie and cold rivulets trickling down her neck and back. Raphe was wearing an unzipped sweatshirt and a long-sleeved black T-shirt with "Believe" stenciled in red letters on the front beneath a skateboarder dropping into a steep bowl. The shirt was completely stuck to his lean, muscled torso by the time they reached the condemned building—six stories of crumbling brick—and its narrow clock tower.

They took the steps two at a time. The front door of the building was completely boarded up, covered with graffiti tags in black, pink, and purple.

"Come on, let's see if there's a side entrance," Raphe said. They ran back down the steps, rounded the corner, and trotted along the east side of the building, careful not to snag their clothes on the barbed wire fence bordering an adjacent empty lot. The side door was boarded over, too, thick wooden planks drilled into the brick wall.

"Let's check the alley." Evangeline ran to the end of the building, turned and entered an eight-foot wide alley with dumpsters and three metal trash bins along one side. Garbage was strewn everywhere—broken bottles, beer cans, decaying food, and soggy trash. The air stank of worms and rotten food.

Evangeline peered up, eyes narrowed against the driving rain. *This was probably once an apartment building. Maybe, it still is for at least one woman.* About twelve feet above them, one of the boards covering a second story window was hanging crookedly.

"Look, Raphe," Evangeline said, pointing. "Help me move a dumpster to stand on, will you?" Holding their breath, they pushed and pulled the least heavy dumpster until it rested beneath the window.

Raphe pulled himself onto the top of the dumpster, then helped Evangeline clamber up. They stood about a foot below the window. Reaching up, Raphe tugged at the board—it was still connected on one side, but loose on the other.

"I'll hold it for you, E, then once you're on the ledge, you can hold it for me," Raphe suggested.

Evangeline crouched beneath the window and then jumped, her hands gripping the crumbling ledge. *Good thing I'm tall after all.* Scrabbling her sneakers along the bricks, she managed to pull herself until she was sitting on the ledge.

"Okay, got it," Evangeline said, wedging her back against the side of the ledge and using her legs to hold the loose board still. Raphe leapt for the ledge and easily pulled himself up beside her. They eased the board back into place, turned, and slid themselves through the opening onto the floor inside.

It was dark. Pitch-black dark once the board had settled back into place. Digging into her jeans pocket, Evangeline pulled out her house keys. On the end of the chain was a tiny flashlight her mom had insisted she keep. Evangeline clicked it on and the narrow beam illuminated an empty room and floor thick with dust. In the corner lay a pile of boards and a can of nails.

"Let's go," she whispered to Raphe and they crept toward the rough door at the far end of the room.

The outer hallway was lined with a fading, threadbare brown and yellow-flowered carpet gnawed through here and there by time or rodents. The musty, thick air was pungent with mold and decay and there were thick cobwebs hanging down from the ceiling. Doors with broken or missing deadbolts lined the hallway every six feet. Raphe and Evangeline stopped at each one, gingerly pushing them open and cringing if they squeaked. Every room was mostly empty—a broken chair, a box of old newspapers, a piece of moldy bread or empty soup can from a squatter long gone.

Approaching the end of the hallway, they reached a stairwell and began to climb. Evangeline stepped cautiously—some of the wooden treads were rotten. Her heart was pounding and even though her skin was cold and clammy, she was also perspiring. What would she say to Samantha? *Who are you? Why did you make us trust you, love you, depend on you if you were only going to betray us? Do you hate us that much? Why? What did my mom and I ever do to you to deserve this?*

"What if she's got a gun or something?" Raphe asked, his thoughts in line with Evangeline's.

"If she does, run. She won't hurt me." But Evangeline wasn't so sure. Detective Morrison thought she was safe, but he could have been wrong.

"I'm not going to leave you," Raphe whispered.

"If she has a gun then one of us will have to go for help."

"You go, then," Raphe said, unwilling to concede.

The next floor up yielded more of the same: empty rooms, some strewn with trash and old upholstered furniture covered in mouse holes and disgusting stains. The next level was also deserted. Evangeline's disappointment grew as they climbed up to the top floor. As scared as she felt, she was also desperate to find Samantha. She had to know why Sam had tried to kill her mother. Evangeline also needed to be the one to turn Sam over to the cops—to feel like she had some control in all this mess. It was the least she could do for her mom. Her godmother had stolen the time she had left with her mom when she'd put her in a coma. *She will pay for that.* Evangeline tried not to think about the fact that she still loved Sam.

Something changed on the top floor. Raphe noticed it first. "The cobwebs—they look like someone's cleared a path through them, don't they?"

The carpet up there was in even worse shape, with large stains and holes that exposed rough floorboards, but Raphe was right. It felt like someone had been there recently. She saw a paw print in the dust and crouched to look at it…the prints were bigger than those a mouse or rat might make. A tinkling bell sounded and suddenly a black cat darted past them, racing down the hall. Raphe slapped a hand over Evangeline's open mouth to stifle her scream. The cat, wearing a collar and bell, disappeared down the staircase.

Evangeline pried Raphe's fingers off her face. "I'm okay," she said, her heart thudding wildly. Swinging her flashlight in the direction the cat had come from, she illuminated a red lacquered door at the far end of the hallway. Unlike the rusty, round doorknobs on all the other doors, this one had a rectangular lever. As they headed toward the door, Evangeline had the distinct sense that everything was about to change.

Taking a deep breath, she reached for the lever and pressed down. Locked.

"Look," Raphe said, pointing to a small, square panel at the base of the door—it was a cat door.

Evangeline knelt beside Raphe and tentatively pushed the plastic flap. Nothing leapt out or grabbed her hand. She put the flashlight in her teeth and poked her head through the opening. Steep wooden stairs led upward. They weren't dust-coated like the ones in the rest of the building. They were spotless and the railings on either side were a smooth stainless steel that reminded Evangeline of her godmother's modern taste.

Feeling a tug around her neck, Evangeline looked down. The chain and key weren't lying flat—the key was pulling on the chain, floating in midair, pulling her forward. Evangeline closed her eyes for a split second. *Stop imagining things—it will only scare you and you're already maxed out!* When she opened her eyes, the key was once again obeying the laws of gravity.

The deafening chimes of the clock tower suddenly began to peal the opening strains of Edelweiss. Caught off guard, Evangeline dropped the flashlight. *It's a sign.* Shoving her sneakers against the floor on the far side of the door, Evangeline forced first one shoulder, then the other, through the cat door, feeling its rough edges scraping along her arms, ribs, and hips.

"What are you doing?" Raphe hissed.

Evangeline used the edge of the first stair to pull the rest of her body through. "I'm letting you in." Quickly she grabbed her flashlight, stood, and unlocked the door, easing it open.

"Don't just go and do something without telling me first," Raphe said, and then he pulled Evangeline close and kissed her. This kiss was longer than her birthday kiss and Evangeline felt her insides start to melt. Raphe's hand rested on her hip, his thumb touching the skin showing beneath her hoodie and lighting it on fire. His lips lingered, gently tugging. They pulled back slowly and then peered up the stairway behind them.

"Ready?" Evangeline whispered, forcing the incredible kiss out of her mind and focusing on the danger ahead.

Raphe nodded. "When did you get so brave?"

"I don't know—I guess when I had to."

They started up the steps, stopping when they reached the door at the top. It wasn't locked. At the very moment Evangeline turned the knob, the clock tower's chimes sounded their last note. *Nothing will ever be the same after I walk through this door. Nothing is ever going to be the same, anyway, is it?*

Evangeline took a breath, opened the door, and crossed the threshold.

CHAPTER TWENTY

Evangeline's flashlight beam illuminated bits of gleaming wood floors, colorful Turkish carpets, sleek black leather couches, and large portraits hung on every wall. Additional paintings and portraits, large and small, oval, square, and rectangular, leaned against the brick. If any place looked like an art agent's lair—like the exact kind of place Samantha would own—this apartment was it.

An elegant mahogany table stood to the left of the entrance with modern silver candlesticks set in the center. Evangeline reached for the box of matches beside the candles. Raphe grabbed her hand.

"What if she's here?" he mouthed.

"I want to find her," Evangeline whispered, pulling her hand free and striking a match on the side of the box.

"Samantha!" she called out, feeling strangely bold and entitled to answers. "Where are you?"

"Jesus," Raphe said, clutching his chest. "You're going to give me a heart attack."

"Sam, come out and face me," Evangeline shouted. "Tell me why you tried to kill my mom! You owe me that!"

There was no answer. Evangeline felt her hopes plummet. "She's not here."

"She could be hiding."

"No. If she was here, she'd show herself."

Grabbing a candlestick, Evangeline walked into the center of the space. Unlike Sam's office and loft, this place felt more lived in—almost inviting. *Does this place reflect the real Samantha?* Walking toward the longest expanse of brick wall, she held the lit candle up to illumine a portrait.

A beautiful woman was depicted in dark oils. She wore the same kind of clothing that Evangeline remembered from a movie about Elizabeth the first—a black velvet dress with a V-shaped bodice decorated with intricate gold embroidery, wide, padded shoulders, and six-inch lace ruffs around her neck and wrists.

The woman's blonde hair also reminded Evangeline of the movie—it was parted down the middle and captured in a wide bun at the nape of her neck. There was a small diamond tiara on the woman's head and several large sapphire rings on her fingers. It was not until Evangeline held the candle higher that she noticed the glint of a necklace resting on the ruff at her neck. It was a radiant black key dangling from a platinum chain.

"Whoa! Isn't that the same necklace you have?" Raphe whispered.

Yes! Evangeline walked to the next portrait—another very pretty woman. She wore a tall, narrow white hat encircled by a black ribbon, with a broad brim hiding all but a few tendrils of platinum-blonde hair. She had a lace ruff around her neck, too, but it was smaller than the first woman's. Her sleeves were tight to her plump arms, and the pale-pink bodice of her ivory dress was embroidered with green flowers. This woman wore no jewelry—except for the same key on a platinum chain. The long fingers of her right hand were touching the carved black stone. For a heartbeat Evangeline thought she saw the woman's fingers caressing the key. She felt her own key pulling toward the painting. *Stop it—it's the flickering candlelight and your own nerves.*

In the next portrait, a different woman wore a yellow dress that matched the color of her hair, which was mostly hidden by a lace cap. The top of her dress was an upside-down triangle with a strategically placed piece of yellow lace covering her cleavage. The rest of the dress looked like the bottom of a tulip, perfectly round and floor-length. This woman's eyes were a lighter blue than the others and slightly downcast. The same key necklace rested in the delicate folds of lace.

Evangeline's mouth was dry as she continued along the row of portraits. The next woman was dressed in a lilac skirt, white off-the-shoulder blouse with large bell-shaped sleeves, and a matching wide-brimmed lilac hat topped with a massive bow. And the key necklace.

"Look how small her waist is," Evangeline said. "She must be wearing the kind of corset Scarlet wore in *Gone With The Wind.*"

"Never saw that flick. Who are these women? What's with the key?"

"I don't know." *Do I?*

In the next portrait, the woman looked like a southern belle with her dark-blonde hair in barrel curls, rosy cheeks, and a flirtatious half-smile playing on a mouth that seemed too wide for her face yet somehow worked to make her even more beautiful. The key necklace was visible on the woman's chest.

From portrait to portrait, four things remained constant: beautiful, blonde hair, blue eyes, and key necklace. The latter rested on the severe pointed collar of a woman wearing an ornate hat in the shape of a comma and a tight bodice of blue silk with enormous puffed sleeves. The glitter of the key was half-buried in a narrow mink stole draped around the neck of another elegant blonde bedecked in a gray silk gown that showed off a curvaceous bust and hips. And, yet again, the necklace was resting on the flat chest of a blonde woman, with thick bangs and chin-length straight blonde hair, bedecked in a gold flapper-style dress.

"I've seen this woman before," Evangeline said, stopping in front of a portrait of a woman wearing an elegant off-the-shoulder beaded gown. The woman stood by a piano, her blonde hair falling in waves, the black key resting above her 36 C-cup cleavage. Evangeline's cheeks burned. "She was an opera singer—Italian, I think. She was spoiled, but nice, too. She died in her bathtub...electrocuted."

Raphe stared at Evangeline, dumbfounded. "E, how the hell do you know that?"

"I dreamt about her." Evangeline shrugged. "And that one," she pointed to a portrait of a woman whose hair was twisted in a low knot and covered by a black velvet riding helmet. Tan riding britches and a matching jacket clothed the woman's tall, athletic frame. The key was resting in the folds of her tailored cotton blouse. "This woman was named Penelope. She wanted to prove to her husband, Louis, that she was still young. She was very jealous of the attention he paid to her daughter's friends...she died in a riding accident."

"You can't possibly know that!"

"I know...but I do."

A portrait on the far wall caught Evangeline's eye and she walked over to it, unable to shake the sensation that she was inside one of her dreams. This woman couldn't have been more than thirty-years-old. Her blonde hair was piled high and held in place with a ruby clip. She wore a lace blouse, the key glinting in its folds. The woman's hands were pressed to-gether in what seemed like a prayer and her nails were painted cherry-red. Evangeline studied her face. She was delicately built, with high cheekbones and wide-set cornflower-blue eyes that appeared very sad. They took on a gleam and suddenly tears were overflowing and running down the woman's cheeks. Evangeline was instantly bathed in a cold sweat.

"Holy crap, do you see that?" She backed away.

"What?" Raphe's voice was concerned. "What, E?"

"That woman in the painting, she's…crying—please tell me you see it, too!"

"What are you talking about?"

"Really! Touch the painting—her cheeks are wet!"

Evangeline stared at the woman's eyes, which met her gaze and then blinked, spilling more tears. "You've got to have seen that!"

Hesitantly, Raphe walked over to the portrait and touched the woman's cheek. "It's dry, E. Look," he held up his fingers. Evangeline touched them—bone dry. She stared at the painting. There were no tears and the woman's eyes were flat paint once more.

"Evangeline, it was just an illusion—probably the candlelight and shadows or whatever."

"I'm losing it, Raphe," Evangeline said, digging shaking fingers into her damp hair. "Seriously. You don't understand."

Raphe put his arms around her. "I want to—try to explain, okay? I want to help."

Evangeline rested her head on Raphe's shoulder, too mortified to let him see her face. "I've dreamt about a lot of these women. The one I thought was crying? I had a nightmare a few days ago that I was that woman and I hung myself in a barn. Here's the crazy part—my mom was having nightmares right before she went into the hospital. She was having crazy delusions, too. I really saw that painting cry. And that's not all."

Disengaging from Raphe's arms, Evangeline took some deep breaths, trying to stay calm, trying to find the words. She started to pace. "Lately I touch things, like my mom's paintings or a mailbox made to look like a waterfall, and it's like they become real for a second. I can feel them and smell them and the waterfall even soaked through my sneaker." She hesitated—afraid to say the words and make what she believed was happening to her real. "I think maybe I have a brain tumor, too." She started to cry and Raphe came up behind her and hugged her tight.

"I don't know what to say, E—I don't get what's going on—but if you are sick, I'll be there for you, okay? I promise—I'm not going anywhere."

Evangeline turned to face Raphe. He looked like he wanted to say more, but didn't. "What?" she asked, wiping her face and feeling totally embarrassed.

"E, the weirdest thing about all this is that all the women in the paintings look they could be related to you." Raphe walked over to one of the portraits and pointed to the woman. "I mean, look at this one. She could be you mom's sister, you know? Do you see it?"

Evangeline recognized Cleo from one of the few photographs her mom had of her grandmother. In the portrait, the prima ballerina was dancing on a stage, sculpted arms outstretched, one lithe leg held high, the other balanced *en pointe* in pink ballet slippers. She was wearing a white leotard and tutu and the key and chain sparkled between her collarbones.

"Yes, that one is definitely related to me. Cleo Theopolis was my grandmother and a famous ballerina. She died in a car crash when my mom was only seventeen and already pregnant with me."

"And look at this!"

Evangeline turned to the portrait Raphe was gaping at and she felt all the air suddenly evaporate from the room. It was her mom. She was dressed in her usual paint-splattered white T-shirt and ripped Levis. Shafts of weak light accentuated the pale-gold of her hair and the brightness of her eyes. Her bowed lips curled into the soft smile she always made when Evangeline came down to breakfast. And resting at her mom's throat was the gleaming black key. Evangeline felt her own throat tighten. *When did mom pose for this painting? Did she even know it was being done? Why was it done?*

"Why?"

"I don't know, E, but this is weirding me out. I think we should get out of here before someone finds us!" He pulled out the asthma inhaler he always carried in his jeans and took a puff.

"Okay, in a minute," Evangeline said.

After seeing her mother's portrait, Evangeline couldn't deny her growing certainty that every single one of the women depicted in these paintings were her ancestors. *Why else would they look like me? Why else would they be wearing the same necklace?* And then she saw the next portrait. *Don't look at it.* But it was too late.

"You look beautiful," Raphe said, staring at the painting Evangeline's mother had made for her sixteenth birthday.

"It was a present from my mom. But it doesn't look anything like me."

"Come with me for a sec." Raphe led her by the hand to a silver filigreed mirror hanging over the front hall table. He took the candle and held it up so she could see her reflection. "What do you see?" he asked.

Wild curls framed a heart-shaped face. Cat-like eyes of storm-cloud-blue drank in the candlelight. Her lips were wide, full, provocative.

"You're beautiful," Raphe said. "I don't know when it happened, but it did."

He's right.

It was as if all the pieces of her jigsaw-puzzle face had fallen into place and found a strange balance. It wasn't a conventional beauty…but the result was the same. Evangeline had always been the ugly duckling—until now. *Why now? Why me?* The key resting on chest seemed to glow in response to her question and she felt it pulsing as if had its own heartbeat.

Backing away from the mirror, Evangeline tripped over the edge of the carpet, her shoulder knocking into an end table, toppling it, and spilling the contents of its half-open drawer. "Still clumsy, though," she said, grinning up at Raphe.

A pile of photographs had fallen out of the drawer and Evangeline turned to pick them up. The shot on top came to life in the flicker of the candlelight. It was a picture of Samantha with two other women and a teenage boy. One woman was Evangeline's English teacher, Mrs. Hopkins. The second woman was athletically built, wearing a tailored gray business suit—it was Beca Petersen, Raphe's mother. Standing beside the three women, his arm casually draped over Sam's shoulder, was Raphe.

"You okay?" Raphe asked, kneeling to help Evangeline up. She scrambled away from him. "E, what's wrong?"

And then he saw the photograph. He stared for a split second and then turned to Evangeline, a confused look on his face. "That's me and my mom with her two best friends, Mrs. Hopkins—which is weird for me at school, so I didn't tell anyone, and Sammy, who works with my mom in sales. I don't know what it's doing here…"

Sammy? That's Samantha! You know her—your mom knows her—and Mrs. Hopkins—she's connected to Sam, too?

"Why didn't you tell me that you knew Samantha Harris?" Evangeline demanded. *Raphe can't be part of this—he can't be—he's my friend—he's more than that.*

Raphe took another puff of his inhaler. "I—I didn't *know* that I knew her until I saw her picture in this morning's newspaper. To me, she's always been Sammy, my mom's partner at work. I never even knew her last name. And I was going to tell you, but everything started to happen so fast. One minute we were in the hospital and the next, we were breaking into this building. E, seriously, I don't know why that picture is here, but you've met my mom—there's no way she'd be involved with Samantha and her fellow freaks."

Stop being paranoid. Raphe cares about me—he helped me, didn't he?—he likes me—he kissed me—he can't be part of this...can he? But why would a guy as cool and cute and popular as Raphe like a girl like me? A small voice in the back of Evangeline's mind whispered. *If things seem too good to be true, they usually are.*

She continued to back away from Raphe, feeling overwhelmed, nauseated, terrified. *Raphe and his mom are friends with Samantha. They know Sam. Their picture's here, in Sam's lair. If it walks like a duck and talks like a duck...they're part of this thing, too.*

Raphe took a step toward Evangeline and she backed further away. "E, stop it! You're looking at me like I'm your enemy. We've been friends for a long time—we're more than friends. I'm here to help you!"

An overwhelming premonition of danger washed over Evangeline. *Raphe helped me break into this building—and it was easy—maybe it was too easy. Is that it? Sam wanted me in her apartment. This, right here, right now, is a trap laid out by Samantha and Raphe so that Sam can try to kill me, too! But why?* Evangeline's mind screamed, scrambling for answers. *It doesn't matter—just get out—NOW!*

Whirling, Evangeline bolted by her grandmother's portrait. "Beware," Cleo cried, one graceful arm darting out of the painting. She felt her grandmother's fingers grasping at her hair, pulling out a few strands as she ducked beneath her pale hand.

A chorus of women's voices shouted after Evangeline: "Beware!" She ignored them all and raced toward the door, leaping down the steps five at a time. Raphe called out to her, but Evangeline didn't dare stop.

Tearing down the hallway of the floor below Sam's, Evangeline heard Raphe's footsteps behind her and accelerated, skidding to the top of the stairs and leaping the first set to the landing in one bound. She landed hard, her right ankle twisting, pain shooting around the joint and up her leg, but she ignored it and plunged down the next flight, using the banister to swing around the corner and—

Evangeline collided into bodies. Hands grasped at her down sweater, hair, shoulders, and they held on tight. A soft cloth was pressed over her nose and mouth. She tried to twist free…it smelled…smelled like…she frantically shook her head back and forth…it smelled like grass and…chemicals…and…and…and then the world went black.

Chapter Twenty-one

Melia and Tristin were making out in the backseat of the black Lexus he'd borrowed from his mother. His hands slid under her sweater, but she pushed them away.

"What's wrong?"

Melia snorted. "Evangeline is going through a world of pain. I'm her best friend and I should be with her. I can't believe she ditched us at the hospital."

"She's probably off somewhere with Raphe," Tristin said, kissing her neck. Melia squirmed away.

"Did you see what she looked like this morning?"

"Yeah, totally hot," Tristin said.

"Wait, what?"

"I meant, totally messed up."

"You think she's hotter than me now, don't you?"

Tristin took Melia's hand. Half-heartedly, she tried to pull it away, but he held firm and spun the silver bracelet he'd given her. The ruby winked in the weak light. "Evangeline isn't my type. You are."

"Bullcrap. She's totally gorgeous and it happened practically overnight," Melia said, frowning. "I had no idea *that* was going to happen."

"Seriously, Melia, she's not my type. Don't you get it? I love you."

"You're just saying that because—"

"Because you're super smart, pretty, fun, and—"

Melia leaned in and kissed him, her tongue twirling inside his mouth.

"Wait," Tristin said, pulling back. "I need to tell you something."

"What is it?"

"Do you really love me?"

"Yes," Melia said. "You know I do."

"Even if I tell you something that's bad?"

"Try me."

"There's something wrong," he began, his voice faltering, and then he pressed on, "and I need your help…"

When Tristin had finished telling Melia his story, she hugged him tightly. "Everyone has their secrets," she began, "even me…"

CHAPTER TWENTY-TWO

Evangeline opened her eyes. She lay curled in the center of a wrought-iron bed covered by a purple quilt, her head resting on a soft down pillow. *Where am I?* The last thing she remembered was running from Raphe. Somehow Raphe was a part of what had happened to her mom. *How do I know that?* Her mind felt slow, fuzzy. *A photograph.* That was it. Raphe's mother, Samantha, Mrs. Hopkins—they were in that photo together.

It all came flooding back and Evangeline's cheeks burned. The whole time she and Raphe had been breaking into the building, searching for Sam, finding her apartment, looking at all those portraits, Raphe had been acting. He was part of Sam's cult and he'd led Evangeline into a trap. She'd been so stupid to think that he was a friend—more than a friend. And she'd told him things she hadn't even shared with Melia.

Raphe said I was beautiful and I believed him. I am such a pathetic cliche. And everything that had happened with the paintings *had* to have been an illusion perpetrated by Raphe, his mother, Samantha, and God knew who else. *Cleo said beware—it wasn't real—but she'd been right.*

Pushing herself into a sitting position was hard. Her twisted ankle was swollen and throbbing. Her head felt like it was filled with lead and her vision was fuzzy around the edges. They'd held a rag to her face and forced her to breathe whatever poison it had been soaked in. *They. Who were they?* Evangeline hadn't been able to see any faces. She'd just felt their hands holding her tightly as she struggled to escape. And then the lights had gone out.

"Why?" Evangeline asked aloud. But there was no answer other than the ticking of a round Mickey Mouse clock set next to a lamp on a bedside table. *I had a clock like that when I was six-years-old. Samantha bought it for me when she took me to Disneyland.* Evangeline looked around the room. The walls were decorated with posters of Pink, Adele, Bonnie Raitt—her favorite musicians. On the table next to the clock was an iPod with earphones. Evangeline picked it up and scrolled through the artists—Wilco, Eminem, Fergie, Kanye West, Beyonce, Rhianna—all music she loved.

Dragging herself to the edge of the bed, she peered at the bookshelf in the corner. Anne Rice, Jodi Picoult, Tim Powers, Joe Hill, Neil Gaiman, Stephen King. Evangeline liked reading all those authors' books. There was also an entire shelf of DVDs from "Talladega Nights" to "28 Days Later" and "Something About Mary." She and Melia had watched "Something about Mary" at least ten times and it still cracked them up. Evangeline felt her eyes burn and fought back a surge of emotion. Crying wouldn't help her now. There was a flat screen TV on the far wall. Music. Books. Movies. *Someone must think I'm going to be here for a long time.*

Evangeline shivered and looked down—she wore only a cotton camisole and underwear. *Where are my clothes? Who took them? Who undressed me?!* Evangeline's face burned. At the foot of the bed were a neatly folded white thermal shirt, Levis and a gray sweatshirt. She yanked on the shirt and jeans, wincing as she put weight on her ankle, and then pulled on the sweatshirt.

Evangeline noticed her mom's beat up guitar resting in the corner of the room and her heart skipped a beat. *How— why was it here?* Her mom could play any song she heard on the radio—Evangeline could, too. When her mom sang, her voice was so pure that Evangeline would stop whatever she was doing to listen. Sometimes they'd harmonize, but lately Evangeline had acted like that was babyish and beneath her—she'd made herself too busy with school, Facebook, texting Melia, and all the other stuff that didn't seem to matter anymore.

Standing on wobbly legs, she limped over to the guitar. Gingerly, she picked it up and returned to the bed. Leaning against the headboard she began to play. It wasn't any song in particular—just the same familiar melody in her mind that she didn't know the words to but that was always there. Humming along with it, she felt her fingers begin to tingle. When the sensation in her hands turned to throbbing and became uncomfortable, Evangeline put the guitar down. She didn't play often and she guessed her fingers weren't tough enough to play for long.

There was a window on the wall to her right and Evangeline stood up again. Strange, her ankle wasn't hurting anymore. She pulled up the jeans and looked at it—the swelling was gone and there was only the pale-blue trace of a bruise. Stranger still, her balance was restored, her head had stopped pounding, and her vision was almost back to normal.

She looked out the window. She was on the second floor of a house and her view was of a backyard bordered by dense forest. There was a greenhouse set against the trees, but she couldn't see inside it because dusk was quickly sliding into darkness. She wasn't on a residential street. That meant no one could hear her yelling for help.

Releasing the lock on the window sash, Evangeline tried to slide the glass up, but it wouldn't budge. The window was nailed shut. "Damn!" Grabbing the desk chair, she took a wild swing, attempting to break the glass. But the chair just bounced off the window. She let the chair clatter to the floor and went over to the bedroom door. She tugged at the knob. It was locked and a set of four bolts ran up in a line above the knob. "Oh, come on!" Grasping the chair again, she bashed it against the door over and over, but the harsh sound after each impact told her that the door that appeared to be wood was actually made of metal. *Is everything a crazy illusion?* Still, she kept swinging until her arms ached. *How am I going to get out of here?*

Finally too exhausted to continue, Evangeline sank onto the wooden floor. *Maybe there's no way out. Ever.* She started hyperventilating and made herself focus on just breathing in and out until the spots and swirls swimming in front of her eyes disappeared. She was being held prisoner. No one knew where she was. There was no one left to care. Samantha had tried to kill her mom. Raphe was somehow involved. Melia didn't know where she was, and her best friend was so in love with and distracted by Tristin that she might not even notice that Evangeline was gone.

What about Dr. Sullivan? Evangeline actually laughed aloud at the idea that her mom's doctor gave a damn where she was. *No one cares.* The feeling of being totally and utterly alone washed over her like a tidal wave. Some freak had locked her in this bedroom. He knew everything about her. He might be a pervert. He might rape her and then he'd probably kill her. *NO. Don't go there or you'll be too paralyzed by fear to help yourself if there's a chance.*

Suddenly, there was the scraping sound of a key in a lock and then bolts being turned and released. One. Two. Three. Four. Evangeline scrambled backward along the floor until she was pressed into the far wall. Wrapping her arms around her legs, she curled into a tight ball. The door eased open…

CHAPTER TWENTY-THREE

Malledy trudged up the steps of the townhouse. Darkness was falling, and after such a long day his bones felt like they were filled with cement—another side effect of the heavier dose of tranquilizers he was taking and the supreme effort required to act like nothing was wrong with him. He took a deep breath, feeling as usual like he couldn't quite fill his lungs. He tried to pull together his thoughts and his plan, and then walked inside.

"I'm home!" Malledy called, shrugging off his backpack and tossing it onto the leather sofa.

Juliette walked out of the kitchen with a bowl of steamed broccoli and brown rice. The smell made Malledy nauseated, but he smiled at the woman who only this morning he'd thought might shoot him. *She should have. She's an Archivist and I'm about to break all the rules. And I'm a threat to Pandora.*

Two reasons to remove me, and both are valid. But the fact that Juliette hadn't killed Malledy had told him everything he needed to know. Juliette still trusted him—not because that was the rational choice—because she loved him. And she was now, at least in the eyes of the Archivists, his willing accomplice. He knew what they would do if they found out. And he assumed that the deadly sect of Pandora would do that, and worse, should Juliette cross them, too. That was why he had to make sure Juliette was never found out.

"Juliette, I need to speak to the leader of Pandora myself," Malledy said, sinking onto a couch and trying not to smell the food his mentor set on the table beside him.

"*Non—impossible*," Juliette said.

"I'm worried about your safety." Malledy's eyes filled with very real tears. "If I can convince the leader to let the girl heal me, then I won't have to steal the box and key for leverage. Please tell her I just want the chance to make my plea." *Please don't become a victim of my disease, too.*

What Malledy didn't say was that only a few hours ago, the last remaining member of the team he'd organized to find the artifacts had confirmed he'd discovered Pandora's lair—thanks to an unsuspecting Juliette. Malledy didn't want that man to make a move until he knew where he stood with Pandora. Until then, he'd continue to play out two scenarios. In the first, Pandora would embrace him and allow the girl to heal him, unwittingly giving him the opportunity to find and acquire Pandora's Box. In the second scenario, either

Juliette, Malledy's man or Malledy himself would find the box and steal it. He'd attain the girl's key to open the box and if wielding the power inside didn't cure Malledy, he'd force the girl, by whatever means necessary, to make him well.

"Please talk to the leader again," Malledy implored. "Tell her that I'll pledge the rest of my life to the Sect."

Juliette hesitated, then nodded. "I'll try. Will you be okay here?"

"Yes." Malledy watched his mentor walk toward the front door. "You know that I love you like a mother?"

"And I love you as a son," Juliette said with a cheerless smile. And then she was gone.

Malledy listened to the silence left in her wake.

"I do love you," he whispered, feeling unbearably sad. "But there's not enough love in the world to keep me from killing you if you stand in the way of my survival."

CHAPTER TWENTY-FOUR

The smell of food made Evangeline's mouth water. A few minutes ago, when the door to her room had swung open, a dirt-encrusted hiking boot had appeared, kicking a tray of food and a thick, leather-bound book into the room. Seconds later, the door had closed with the bolts thrown shut. Evangeline had missed her opportunity to escape—she'd been too afraid to move.

The meal was curried chicken over brown rice—one of Evangeline's favorites. She knew that she shouldn't eat it, though—it was surely poisoned. Picking up the book, she climbed back onto the bed.

The leather was buttery soft and the pages were yellowed parchment, brittle and wavy with age. There was a cord of red silk marking a page. Evangeline flipped to it. The writing was tiny and composed of swooping black letters that looked like the calligraphy on wedding invitations. Evangeline began to read:

The Gods created the first woman, Pandora, endowing her with spellbinding traits and magical abilities, and sent her down from Mount Olympus with a golden box. Inside the box were five Furies meant to plague mankind for their crime of accepting stolen fire from Mount Olympus. But Hope was also placed inside the Box by Hera, Zeus' queen, because the Goddess believed that without Hope mankind would lose the will to survive.

At the last moment, Hades, God of the Underworld, gave Pandora a key fashioned out of an enchanted obsidian stone. Should Pandora realize that the box she carried contained the Furies, she could use the key to lock it. Once locked, no force of Man or Nature could open the box—only Pandora and the key.

Pandora arrived at the home of Epimetheus and he readily accepted the first woman. However, he refused to open the gift she'd brought to him, because his brother, Prometheus, had told him never to accept a gift from the Gods. Driven by insatiable curiosity, Pandora opened the golden box herself, releasing the Furies.

And the Gods cheered as the terrifying drama unfolded. But their elation was short-lived because the God Hermes had given Pandora the gift of cunning. When she realized what she'd done by opening the box, Pandora slammed the lid and locked it, trapping Annihilation, the fifth and most devastating Fury inside.

Furious that the fifth Fury he'd created wasn't released, Zeus hurled a curse down on Pandora. For the crime of trapping the fifth Fury, Pandora would violently die when she was in the prime of her life.

The hairs on her arms rose and she shivered. She touched the key—it felt as ice-cold as she suddenly did. *This is just a made-up story that some freak created to scare me.* Turning the page, Evangeline read on:

For her own amusement, the Goddess Athena added to Zeus' curse. She decreed that it would apply to any female descendant Pandora might give birth to before her death.

Slamming the book shut, Evangeline grabbed the key, intending to rip it off. She didn't believe anything she'd read was true, but it still seriously freaked her out. An intense pain shot through her palm and she let go of the key, looking down in shock. Her palm was seared—burned in the shape of the key! *This is totally crazy.*

Suddenly, the bolts were being turned in rapid succession. Evangeline's head snapped up just as someone slipped through, their back to her. The bolts were thrown again and a figure turned to face her.

"Melia!" Evangeline leapt from her bed and wrapped her arms around her best friend, holding too tight but unable to let go. "They got you, too? What do they want from us?"

"We want you to protect the box, Evangeline," Melia replied calmly.

CHAPTER TWENTY-FIVE

Evangeline felt like the floor beneath her had fallen away. Up was down. Right was wrong. *Could it be that Melia was one of them, too?*

"Don't look at me like that," Melia implored. "E, try to understand, okay? I was born into this, too—me and my real mom, and her mother before her. We all protect the descendants.

"Do you hear yourself, Melia?" Evangeline asked, bile rising in the back of her throat. "The *descendants* of what?"

"Of Pandora."

"Oh, please! You are out of your mind!" Evangeline backed away from the girl she'd loved like a sister—the girl who was now a stranger. *I am not a descendant of Pandora.*

She noticed Melia was wearing flip-flops. *Indoor shoes. Shoes you leave in a house you visit often—where you're comfortable and at home.* There was a gold ring on her second right toe.

"We all have this toe ring. It's inscribed with the word, *Pandora*," Melia said. "That's our Sect."

"Our *Sect*? You mean a cult for you, Samantha, and Raphe—and who else?"

Melia looked startled and confused. "What are you—just hear me out, okay? Please?"

"Why bother? I don't believe that a mythical box created by fictional Greek Gods ever existed, let alone Pandora and—"

"And her descendants," Melia finished. "But what if you're wrong, E? What if the box did exist? What if it still does? What if a devastating fifth Fury remains inside—like you just read about? Don't you think there are people in the world who'd want to get their hands on it?"

"Okay, I'll play along with your sick game. There's a big bad Fury around and some people want it. What people?"

"Their names don't matter, E. They work for companies, governments, and dictators in countries that want to manipulate the world for money and power or in the name of religion."

"Right." Evangeline held up the gleaming black key. "So, go ahead. Just take this key if it's what you freaks think it is. Lock up your precious box. Just let me go!"

"It doesn't work that way. The box is already locked. Only a descendant of Pandora can unlock it. If any of us tried, the key wouldn't work."

"Then someone will just have to break it open if they want whatever's inside so badly."

"It can't be cut, burned, crushed, or sliced open with a laser—*nothing* can open the box but the key and you."

"Bull."

Melia met Evangeline's angry gaze. "I'm not lying to you, I swear. You wear the key, but the truth is that you *are* the key. Whatever happens to the Fury is totally up to you. And you're in danger because of it."

Evangeline had had enough. She picked up the lamp on the bedside table, yanked out the cord, and wielded the brass base like a weapon. "Let me out of this room!"

"You're going to hit me with that? Really? Don't be insane!"

Evangeline took a step forward. Her best friend didn't back up.

"Screw you, Evangeline! I've been dealing with this bull my whole life. You have no idea! It's time for you to shoulder at least some of the load!"

Evangeline took another step forward.

Melia snorted. "I'm a black-belt, don't forget."

That was true. Evangeline had always wondered why someone as girly as Melia cared about karate lessons. Melia used to say that it gave her a great ass. *I bought that lie, too.*

"Don't make me take that lamp away, because I'll do it," Melia said. "I'll do anything to protect the key, box, and *you*. That's what I'm trained to do. And even if you get past me, which is highly unlikely, there are a bunch more women outside that door and they're tougher than you could ever imagine."

"I hate you!" Evangeline said, dropping the lamp to the floor.

"Great!" Melia snapped. "That's just great! I've spent my entire life trying to protect you and Olivia."

"Don't you *dare* say my mother's name like you care! Your cult tried to kill her."

Melia rolled her eyes. "Look, E, you're not going anywhere right now so why not shut up for a few minutes?"

Evangeline backed into the far wall, arms crossed. Melia was right, for the moment there was no escape. "Go ahead," she said. *But I can guarantee I won't believe a word you say.*

Melia sat down on the edge of the bed. "*Pandora* is the *cult* you're talking about. Despite the Gods' protests, the Goddess Hera started our Sect to create a group of women devoted to helping Pandora and her descendants protect the box and keep the final Fury inside."

"That makes no sense," Evangeline scoffed. "Why would Hera do that if the Gods wanted the fury released?"

"Probably because if the fifth Fury was liberated, the drama of Pandora and the box might end. The Gods were enjoying the show. And they like a show that can go on as long as possible, I assure you."

Evangeline knocked the back of her head against the wall, hard. *Nope, not dreaming.* "I'm not a descendant of Pandora."

Fixing her with a determined look, Melia pressed on. "I don't know when the descendants of Pandora lost the thread of their own story. But now Pandora chooses to keep them in the dark about their ancestry, their role, and the curse."

"Probably because if someone knew what you wing-nuts were up to they'd have you arrested or committed!"

"Or because," Melia shot back, "we can't risk what a descendant would do if she learned about the curse. The bottom line is that we alone protect descendants from anyone who wants to hurt them or possess the artifacts—the box and the key."

Evangeline pressed palms against her temples. "Melia, you need serious mental intervention. You've been brainwashed to believe in a fantasy based on some mythology about people and Gods who never existed. There are probably specialists who can fix you with the help of powerful anti-psychotic drugs."

"Look, E, whatever. Face it, you've got it great. You've all got beauty and mad skills like singing, painting, dancing. And there's a whole devoted group of women who pull every string to make certain that your life stays blessed with whatever you desire."

"You mean my *abbreviated* life. Don't forget, descendants are supposed to die in their prime."

Melia frowned. "I haven't forgotten, but there are people who would gladly trade their ugly, boring lives for the life you, Olivia, Cleo, Penelope, Anna, Helen, and all those who came before them got to live."

"Right. And seeing as I have nothing to do with all of this, what if I want a boring life?"

Melia met Evangeline's challenging gaze. "Too bad."

"Says you."

"Stop being such a selfish brat—this is bigger than you, whether you believe it or not! Evangeline, the fifth Fury is *Annihilation*. That means total obliteration with no trace, no signature, and no one to blame. If whoever possesses the fifth Fury can harness its power, they will get away with murder and never be caught. They can blame any person or country or fanatic religion for their actions and there'll never be a way to prove differently. Annihilation, Evangeline. Poof—a whole population or an entire country gone."

Melia's eyes had taken on a fanatic gleam and her cheeks were flushed. *How can you argue with someone who's been brainwashed her entire life? You can't.* "How long is your cult going to keep me locked up?"

"Sect. I don't know."

They're not planning to let me go, Evangeline suddenly realized. *How can they? I know too much about them now.*

Melia approached swiftly and wrapped her arms around Evangeline before she could stop her.

"They're listening," Melia whispered. "Look, just relax. I'll come back tonight—we'll get out of here together, OK?"

She let go and backed toward the door. "Eat the food, E, it's not drugged. They wouldn't risk hurting you."

Melia stepped out of the room and shut the door behind her. The bolts thudded back into place.

CHAPTER TWENTY-SIX

Juliette turned off the blaring radio that Malledy had tuned to his favorite rap station and drove back to the townhouse in silence. She'd done all that she could; said all that she could think of; promised, pledged, and only stopped short of begging because she didn't want the leader of Pandora to see her desperation. Desperation would signal that Juliette was capable of anything, even betrayal.

It was raining again, as it seemed to always do in the Godforsaken city of Portland. Juliette focused on the road—she hadn't been behind the wheel of a car for many years and driving didn't come naturally. It was just one of the many things she'd given up when she'd become an Archivist. The others included marriage, a family, and most, if not all, of her morals. Not that she'd clung to many principles as a member of Pandora, either. Both Sects believed that the end justified the means, although Pandora clung to somewhat higher ground as to the reasons why they would deceive and murder to achieve their goals.

Juliette's cell phone rang and she dug into her purse while keeping her eyes on the highway. "*Allo?*"

"I'm sorry," Pandora's leader said, "but the answer is no."

"To Malledy meeting with you?" Juliette marveled at how calm her voice sounded despite her racing pulse.

"To everything. We simply can't risk it."

Juliette swallowed, hearing the dry click of her throat. "I understand."

"Do you?"

"Yes. Pandora is forever. Everything else can be sacrificed—even Malledy's life. I understand."

There was a pause and then the leader spoke again. "We're gathering."

"I'll be there." Juliette hung up and signaled to exit the highway. She swung off and turned to get on the highway going back the way she'd come.

CHAPTER TWENTY-SEVEN

The greenhouse was bathed in an orange glow. The thirty-one robed women of Pandora stood in a circle chanting in ancient Greek.

"Let's begin," the leader said, holding up her hand.

"Samantha, she shouldn't have given Evangeline the book." Melodie Hopkins glared at Melia.

"Planning to send me to detention?" Melia asked. "Too bad. I'm your equal here."

"Why did you do it, Melia?" Samantha asked, her cat-like eyes narrowed.

"You drugged Evangeline and locked her up! She's freaking out. She has the right to know what's going on."

"You act like you weren't a part of our decision," Melodie said. "*You're* the one who warned us that she'd left the hospital."

"Did I say to hunt her down, chloroform her, kidnap her, and lock her up?" Melia shouted.

Samantha held up a hand again. "Giving Evangeline the book was a decision that should've been made by all of us, Melia."

The women shifted uneasily. The book was a sacred chronicle of Zeus' Curse and contained the history of every descendant. No individual outside the Sect or any descendant of Pandora had ever seen, let alone read, the book. The knowledge it contained was dangerous for a multitude of reasons, including the risk that someone might seek the box and key for their own gain or a descendant might try to break from her destiny in defiance or fear.

"Evangeline wasn't ready to learn about the curse," Lacie said. Evangeline would've been astounded to see Goth girl right now. She wasn't wearing her usual white makeup and black eyeliner—she had pretty gray eyes and olive-toned skin.

"You think there's some way to backtrack from the road we've gone down?" Melia snapped at her classmate.

Belinda O'Neill, a brunette bombshell and Melia's stepmother, put a restraining hand on Melia's shoulder.

"Don't start acting like a mother now," Melia said, shaking free. "I helped you seduce my dad so that I'd be raised by a member of Pandora after my mother's death, but that doesn't mean I like you."

"Enough!" Samantha said. "Regardless of your perception about the road we've gone down, Melia, you should've let the Sect decide the most prudent course of action."

"And waited? Sam, she's freaking scared out of her mind!" Melia stepped out of the circle to take in the entire Sect, looking from one powerful woman to the next. "Olivia is dying. Evangeline saw Sam—the only other adult she trusted and loved—trying to suffocate her mom. And she thinks I've been lying to her for her whole life."

"You have," Melodie pointed out. Melia returned to her place in the circle of women.

"*Alors!* We are all missing the forest for the trees," Juliette said. "Evangeline *must* remain locked safely away, at least for a time. But more importantly, we must make sure the box isn't close enough for her to obtain."

Samantha fixed a laser gaze on Juliette. "Why?"

"She's an angry teenager. There's no telling what she'd do if she had the box. At the very least she could use it to manipulate *us*."

"Juliette's right," Belinda said.

"Is the box close by?" Juliette asked.

"It's safe." Samantha turned to face Melia. "We're going to depend on you to help Evangeline through this."

"No."

There was a collective intake of breath. "Excuse me?" Samantha said.

"I said, no," Melia replied. The silence in the greenhouse was deafening.

"You can make the difference between Evangeline being miserable or accepting the boundaries of her new life. Why would you decline?"

"How can I help my best friend believe everything I've told her when I'm not sure *I* believe all of it?"

The women began to speak at once, voices raised in anger and protest.

Melia continued. "I was born into all this. No one asked me if I wanted to be a member of Pandora."

"It's an honor," Melodie said.

"Right. I'm expected to die a member of Pandora and that'll probably happen protecting Evangeline and the artifacts. But I've never even seen the box. I honestly don't know if it exists. So I can't help you because I won't lie to Evangeline anymore. *I won't do it.*"

"Only a handful of our Sect knows the location of the box," Belinda said. "That's for your own safety. Melia, the more you know, the more dangerous it is for both you and the descendant."

"You *need* me," Melia said to Samantha. "And *I* need to know that what I'm about to do to my best friend is the right thing."

"So, are you telling us you didn't believe in Pandora when you took your vows?" Samantha grasped Melia's hand, turning it over to expose the pink lines in the shape of a P recently carved into her skin.

Melia pulled her hand away. "I guess not."

"Step forward if any of you feel the way Melia does," Samantha commanded. A handful of the younger initiates looked uncertain but only one other member of Pandora stepped forward— Juliette. Samantha's eyes betrayed her surprise.

"I need to know beyond all doubt that Malledy's death is justified," Juliette said to the leader. "Please." She locked eyes with Samantha. "Forgive my weakness."

"Very well." Samantha said. "Come with me, both of you."

"You *can't* be serious," Melodie scoffed, her eyes wide with disbelief.

"If Melia and Juliette weren't such valuable members of Pandora I would choose a different course," Samantha explained. "But the truth is that we need them." She turned and led the way out of the greenhouse without looking back. The three women entered the cedar-shingled house through the back door, crossed the hallway, and climbed a curved, wooden staircase to the second floor, passing the room where Evangeline was imprisoned.

At the end of the hallway was a sewing room jammed floor to ceiling with bolts of cloth, spools of thread, and stacks of brightly colored patches meant to be sewn together to fashion quilts. Once Juliette and Melia were inside, Samantha shut the door behind them.

"Are you certain that this is what you want?" Samantha asked. "Because the knowing is a burden that is at times almost beyond bearing."

"Yes," Melia and Juliette replied in unison.

CHAPTER TWENTY-EIGHT

It was raining so hard, the windshield wipers made little difference and only the yellow lines on the road gave any guidance. Dr. Sullivan glanced at the dashboard—it was 12:37 AM.

"How did this happen," he asked softly.

A neon-red glow indicated an all-night liquor store a block ahead. Dr. Sullivan signaled and slowed, then parked in front of the store. "It happened because I just want to forget." He got out.

Running through the downpour, Dr. Sullivan passed a hunched-over kid in a soaking wet sweatshirt and jeans walking in the opposite direction. He did a double-take.

"Hey, kid, what're you doing out here?"

Raphe turned, his face wet, pinched, uncertain.

"I saw you at the hospital. You're a friend of Evangeline. I'm Ms. Theopolis' doctor—Tim Sullivan?"

"Oh, yeah, I remember." Raphe shivered. "My car broke down a few miles back. I'm trying to find an open gas station or a mechanic or something."

"Have you called your parents? They're probably worried sick."

Raphe shook his head. "My mom's out of town."

Dr. Sullivan glanced over his shoulder at the liquor store, hesitating. "I can give you a ride home," he finally said. "What's your name?"

"Raphe. Thanks, that would be great—I'm freezing."

They climbed back into the Volvo and Dr. Sullivan turned up the heater. "Where to?"

Raphe looked down at his palms. "78 Prentiss Street—it's near Forest Park."

Dr. Sullivan reached beneath the seat for his thermos. Resting it between his knees, he unscrewed the top and took a swallow, tried for a second one, and came up empty.

"My dad had a thermos just like that one," Raphe said. "He kept vodka in his cause he figured my mom wouldn't be able to smell it on his breath. She kicked him out. Crazy hunh?"

"Ah…Not that it's your business, but this is water."

"Yeah, whatever. Look, Evangeline told me what happened to your family, doc, and I'm really sorry. I just figured—" Raphe shrugged. "Anyway, I'm sorry—about it all."

Dr. Sullivan pulled away from the curb and tightened his grip on the steering wheel.

"Raphe, do you know where Evangeline is? I was supposed to drop her off at the police station this morning after she visited her mom, but I couldn't find her."

"Are the police looking for her?" Raphe asked.

"Detective Morrison hasn't put out an Amber Alert or anything, but, yes, they're looking. She's not in trouble. We just need to make sure she's safe. You understand that, right?"

Raphe drummed his fingers on the dash—fast, repetitive. "Yeah, I understand. Sammy—um, I mean Samantha—and the rest of them are still out there."

"Do you know where Evangeline is?"

Raphe peered through the rivulets of rain cascading down the windshield, brow wrinkled. "I saw them take her," he said, his voice nearly a whisper.

"What the hell?" Dr. Sullivan glanced over at Raphe. "What are you talking about?"

"Me and Evangeline, we found Samantha's apartment in a condemned building. There were all kinds of weird things in there—portraits of women who I think were all Evangeline's ancestors—and photographs. Evangeline freaked and ran away—"

"But, why?"

Raphe shrugged. "By the time I caught up to her they were carrying her down the stairs."

"They, who?" Dr. Sullivan demanded.

"I'm not exactly sure, but I know she was unconscious."

Dr. Sullivan shook his head to clear it. "Why didn't you stop them?"

"There were too many."

"Why didn't you call the police?"

Raphe looked down at his fingernails—they were bitten to the quick. "Because."

"I'm running out of patience. Because why?"

Raphe turned in his seat to look at the doctor. "Because one of them was my mother."

CHAPTER TWENTY-NINE

"You want this room to be your grave?" Melia asked.

"Why should I trust you?" They stood in Evangeline's darkened room. It was almost one o'clock in the morning and the sounds of the house had long since faded as her jailors retired for the night. Evangeline had been asleep, too, in the white flannel PJs her captors had left in a dresser drawer. Melia's hand over her mouth had woken her.

Do I want this room to be my grave? What's she talking about? Who is Melia, really? She's lied to me our whole lives. "Were you ever really my friend?"

"Oh, E." Melia gave Evangeline a look of pure exasperation. "This is not the time."

Crossing her arms, Evangeline sat back down on the edge of her bed. "You're popular. You could've hung out with the jocks or the cheerleaders, but you stayed with me. Did they make you do it?"

"No," Melia said, "and yes. E, I'm just a kid, too. There were times when I got sick of looking out for you, but I also loved you like a sister. No matter what you think, I still do. And in case you haven't looked in the mirror lately, you're not a geek anymore. You're stunning—kind of a cross between Uma Thurman and Angelina Jolie but with way better hair."

"Really?" Evangeline ran a hand through her hair. "How'd that part happen, M?"

"The beautiful part? I don't know. Honestly, I wasn't expecting it, either."

"Do you mind?"

Melia's eyes locked with Evangeline's. "Yes."

"That might be the first true thing you've ever said to me."

"If that's what you think," Melia whispered, turning toward the door, "then I'm out of here."

"No, wait! Will you...will you take me to the hospital to see my mom?"

"If you don't believe in anything I'm saying and think everything I'm doing for you is BS, why should I bother continuing to help you? Why should I bother taking you to see your mom?"

I have to do something—trust someone—take control of my own life. "Because a few days ago we were best friends," Evangeline said, feeling a sense of emptiness and loss. "I have to trust someone…and the only *someone* I have left is *you*. So, let's go—please!"

Melia grabbed Evangeline's arm and half led, half pushed her toward the door. "Stephanie had the first shift guarding your room. She's a coffee fiend, so I brought her a latte and drugged it with my step-monster's Valium. She won't stop us!" Melia chuckled.

"Wait—I've got to get dressed."

"Stephanie passed out ten minutes ago, but I don't know how long she'll sleep. You're fine—we'll get you some clothes and shoes later, okay?"

They snuck by Stephanie asleep in a chair, wearing a black track suit and Nikes, her chin was bobbing on her chest and her hand resting on an unsheathed knife in her lap. They crept down the hall and Melia paused at the last door on the right.

"I thought we were getting out of here," Evangeline whispered.

"Quiet," Melia mouthed. They slipped into a sewing room overflowing with bolts of fabric. Melia tiptoed to the far wall and pulled up the window shade. In the weak light of a crescent moon partially obscured by rain clouds, Evangeline could make out a large oak tree. Unlocking the window, Melia inched it open, wincing as it caught and scraped. She and Evangeline forced the window all the way open. Balanced in the crook of the oak, sat Tristin, wearing a black jacket and dark jeans. He held up a hand in greeting.

"What's he doing here?" Evangeline hissed.

"Helping me break you out of this place."

Reaching behind a bolt of checkered fabric, Melia withdrew a small golden box which seemed to be giving off an inviting pale-pink glow. Evangeline couldn't help staring at it and she reached for the box. Melia shook her head and placed the box in her backpack. Evangeline felt both disappointed and strangely relieved to see it disappear.

"Go ahead," Melia urged. "You first."

Evangeline climbed onto the windowsill. The tree was a good six feet away. "I can't," she said, looking down at the two-story drop.

"It's a leap of faith or you'll be back in that room, locked away for I don't know how long."

"Come on!" Tristin urged. Evangeline pushed off into his waiting arms.

CHAPTER THIRTY

The trail that led through the forest was narrow, the pine and oak trees dense, and sharp rocks and brambles cut Evangeline's bare feet. But she pressed on, determined to put as much distance as possible between herself and the cult that'd kidnapped her. *Run. Get away. Get to the hospital. Get to mom before it's too late!*

None of them spoke and the only sound was the whisper of leaves, an owl's insistent hoot, and their labored breath.

"I've got…to stop…for a minute. Please." Evangeline was panting after almost an hour of hard running, hands on her thighs, trying to regain her breath. A cramp burned across her side and her feet throbbed.

"We need to keep moving," Melia said, looking nervously behind them.

Tristin put his hand on Evangeline's back. "Just give her a second."

Melia violently shook her head. "Tristin, you don't understand! The people who're coming after us, they won't think twice about killing you. And I'm not sure what they'll do to *me*."

"You okay?" Tristin asked, crouching beside Evangeline.

"No—yeah, but my feet are trashed and I just need a few minutes...to catch my breath."

"We don't have a few minutes," Melia said. "Get moving—now!"

Feeling terrified and angry at the same time, Evangeline stared at her friend. "Okay, then, give me your sneakers."

"You're such a spoiled brat," Melia lashed out. "Everything isn't always about you, you know!"

"That's not what your freakish cult believes." Evangeline felt sick hearing the fury in her own tone. *We've never fought like this before. But then, I'm not the same girl I was a few days ago and Melia isn't the best friend I thought she was, either.*

"I am *so* sick of taking care of you!" Melia pushed Evangeline in the chest so she stumbled backward.

"And *this* is taking care of me?" Evangeline asked, looking down at her bloody feet. She knew she shouldn't be pissing Melia off so much, but she couldn't help it.

Color rose in Melia's cheeks and her eyes narrowed. "You want to do this? Okay, let's do this. Ask me why my mother died. Ask me!"

"She died in a car accident. You told me about it when we were little kids."

"I was in that car, too!"

"What?" Evangeline's stomach twisted in knots. "You never—"

"No, I never told you because I wasn't *allowed* to tell you. My mom *purposely* plowed into a car that was being driven by a man trying to kill *your* mother to get control of the key! I was in the car and my door was the impact point. My own mother didn't care that I might've died. We spun out from the crash and the other side of the car hit a telephone pole. The impact broke my mom's neck."

"Oh my god, Melia, I'm really sorry—I—"

"Shut up, E, I'm not done! Do you know how my grandmother died?"

Evangeline shook her head. *Please stop.*

"She was shot to death protecting Cleo, *your* grandmother. Ever since I can remember I've been told that it's my *destiny* to do the same thing—my *destiny* to risk my life and be ready and willing to die for *you*. And I was, but that shouldn't mean I don't get to live a great life, too."

"I never asked you to die for me," Evangeline said quietly. She felt tears welling up and struggled not to cry. "I never asked for any of this."

"Evangeline, just stop feeling sorry for yourself and do something for someone else. Help Tristin."

"What are you talking about?" Evangeline was caught completely by surprise. *Help Tristin? What could Melia's boyfriend possibly need from me?* "Help Tristin?"

"There's something wrong with him," Melia said. "E, it was really hard for Tristin to tell me—he only did because he loves me. He wanted me to know before it was too late—so we could say goodbye. Tristin has a fatal disease. He didn't know about you—your abilities as Pandora's descendant—but I told him because I love him. You can understand that, can't you? E, he needs you to heal him. You can at least do that."

Wiping away her tears with the back of her hand, Evangeline stared at her friend. "Heal him? I'm not a doctor, Melia. Is that why you helped me get away—you think I have some magical powers that I can use to fix your *boyfriend?*"

"You *do*," Tristin said, stepping toward Evangeline. "You're a descendant whether you believe it or not. Demeter gave the original Pandora the gift of making anything grow and heal. I never thought those powers could pass to Pandora's descendants, but they have. You have the power to heal me, Evangeline, I know you do!"

"E, if our friendship ever meant anything you'll do this." Melia was starting to sound desperate.

"Do this?" Evangeline's voice was calm. She wanted to scream, but was too afraid that members of Pandora were already hunting for them. She'd be damned if she'd give away her whereabouts now. She also knew that if she began to scream she might never stop.

"E, Tristin is the only person in my whole freaking life who has ever put me first. And he's been watching out for you, too. He didn't just help me get you out of that house; he has a plan to keep Pandora from coming after us."

Melia shrugged off her backpack, unzipped it, and pulled out the golden box. "E, this is Pandora's Box. As long as we possess both the box and key, the Sect will have to leave us alone."

Tristin nervously shifted from foot to foot as he watched Evangeline's reaction.

"Why? Because you plan to threaten them with opening that thing?" Evangeline was feeling like Alice in Wonderland hurtling down the rabbit hole. She struggled to ignore the fact that she once again felt strangely drawn to the box. *Why can't I seem to look away it? Why do I want to touch it so badly? I have to get out of here. I have to get away from them. They're both insane.*

With sheer force of will, Evangeline tore her eyes from the golden box and inched away from Melia and Tristin so she could have enough space to turn and run without being caught. Behind her, a rushing creek flowed through the woods, overflowing its banks in places due to the abundant rains. Evangeline retreated until her heels sank into the creek's muddy edge. She'd have to wade through in order to get away. The water rushed and gurgled against rocks—it sounded fast and deep. *How many people will I be running from after I bolt?*

"Don't!" Tristin had a silver revolver aimed at Evangeline.

A scream tore from Evangeline's lips.

"Stop moving or I'll shoot you."

"Tristin! What are you doing? Melia launched herself between Evangeline and Tristin. "Tristin, don't! You don't need—"

The gun went off—the sound more of a sharp hiss than an explosion.

Melia stared down at the hole in the center of her sweater and then her knees buckled and she fell onto the forest's floor.

"You," Tristin said calmly. "My name is Malledy, not Tristin, and I don't need you anymore."

CHAPTER THIRTY-ONE

Melia was lying on her back, tears streaming from the corners of her eyes, down her temples, and into her hair. Evangeline crouched next to her friend, trembling hands hovering over her body. "Melia!—Oh god—oh god—oh god—tell me what to do!!"

With a laugh, Malledy picked up Pandora's Box from where it gleamed in the dirt beside Melia's crumpled body. It was only a small box—no more than six inches square—but the final Fury housed inside gave it a deadly weight that he could feel trying to creep into his bones. The swirls carved into the rose-colored gold were mesmerizing and for a moment, Malledy let his eyes trace the ancient carvings before forcing them away.

I am so close. I have the talismans; I have the descendant; I will be healed! And then... Malledy's mind sprinted, whirled, twisted upside down and inside out, and arrived at a monumental realization. "And then," he murmured, his tone overflowing with awe and reverence, "I will become a modern day God." *How could I have missed it? There's no difference between me and the ancient Gods of Greece—not anymore. And the world needs me—mankind needs me to save it from itself!*

Malledy yanked the silver bracelet off Melia's wrist, leaving only tarnish marks where the metal had touched her skin. He flicked the gun's safety back on. Juliette had given him the gun for his own protection. He'd promised only to use it if he was in mortal danger and never, ever, to threaten the life of the descendant. *Promises were made to be broken.*

Malledy grabbed Evangeline's upper arm and yanked her to her feet. She was blubbering and shrilly screamed at his touch, but he clamped a hand over her mouth and wrapped his other arm around her waist.

"Don't hurt her, Tristin," Melia called weakly.

"Try to catch up, Melia. The name's Malledy." He moved his mouth to Evangeline's ear. "I never loved her. It's you I wanted—it was always you."

Evangeline struggled to free herself, but Malledy's grip was iron. In a lightning swift motion, Malledy slid the silver bracelet onto her wrist. He couldn't be sure how long it would take the ruby to work. It had only taken seconds for the powerful gem from the scepter of Aphrodite to bewitch Melia to profess her undying love for him. It had made

Melia unbelievably willing, as well as entirely blind, to his true plans.

"Evangeline, I know you're freaked out, but Melia wasn't really your friend. She told me everything about who you really are. She told me about the key and box. She sold you out to a guy she'd only known for a few months."

Evangeline thrashed and twisted her head, managing to bite down on Malledy's thumb.

"*Merde!*" He loosened his hold just enough for Evangeline to squirm free and scramble away.

"Melia! Help me!"

"Run—run, E!"

Malledy managed to catch the cuff of her pajama leg and jerk her back into his embrace. She bucked, her head catching his chin and snapping his teeth together. He could taste the blood in his mouth.

"Stop fighting me, you witch!"

"Go to hell!" Evangeline growled, ripping the bracelet from her wrist. She stamped down on Malledy's foot, once more loosening his grip enough for her to break free. She stumbled and started to run.

Diving forward, Malledy tackled Evangeline, driving her face into the dirt and the breath from her lungs. She kept struggling, even as she gasped for air.

"Stop it!" Malledy demanded. *The bracelet didn't work on her! Amazing!* "Listen to me! I'm not going to kill you. Melia wasn't lying—I need your help."

"Don't—don't believe—anything he—says!" Melia weakly cried.

Evangeline clawed at Malledy's face, trying to find his eyes. He swore as her nails tore into his skin.

Made incredibly powerful by his pain, adrenaline, and the desperate need for self-preservation, Malledy twisted Evangeline's body, straddled her torso, and backhanded her. For just a second, her eyes went blank and she licked at the blood on her split lip. Malledy watched for a moment and then, driven by a sudden, overwhelming rage, dragged Evangeline toward the creek.

His disease-riddled mind scrambled for a plan even as his fury burned bright. He'd hold her under the water until she passed out. *Does this make sense? Yes!* After she was unconscious, he'd carry her to his car. Once he had her tied up somewhere safe and quiet, he'd get her to heal him—whether she wanted to or not. And if that didn't work, he'd have her open the box and do it himself. *Perfect sense.*

He dragged Evangeline through the mud to the edge of the rushing water. He pinned her down with his knees and took hold of her thick hair readying to force her head below the torrent. Evangeline fought as hard as she could, her fingers continuing to claw at Malledy's face. He kept out of reach and began to force her head into the water.

Suddenly the dark-blue of her eyes altered, taking on the look of an electric night sky just before lightning flashed. And Evangeline began to hum. The tune was strangely beautiful.

And then it changed, as if someone flipped a switch and the song was running backwards. The sweet notes now sounded all wrong—flat, sharp, grating. Malledy shook his head and plunged Evangeline's face into the icy creek.

In the weak moonlight Malledy could see Evangeline's panicked face, her eyes were impossibly wide, darting left and right—searching desperately for an escape. A vein in the center of her forehead bulged and her lips were peeled back in a terrified grimace. *Just pass out, damn it, so we can get out of here!*

In a burst of strength, Evangeline grabbed fistfuls of Malledy's jacket, and attempted to pull herself up. Grunting, he pushed her deeper under the surface until her head hit the rocky bottom of the creek. Evangeline's visage took on a silvery-glow. The pupils of her eyes abruptly dilated and morphed into luminous black pearls. She began to hum again. *How does she have the breath left? She is a sorceress!* It was the same discordant tune she'd hummed moments before. Malledy could hear the notes, even though Evangeline's head was submerged. *How is this possible?*

"Stop it! Stop it!" Malledy hissed, but the melody grew louder and he imagined he could feel it slithering along his exposed skin like a thousand tiny, deadly snakes. "STOP IT!"

Slowly, Evangeline's struggles eased and then ceased entirely. Her song drifted away, replaced by the rustling of the leaves in the trees. Malledy watched Evangeline's hands slide down to rest lifelessly on her belly. Her face, framed by floating tendrils of hair, was a watery mask and her eyes were glazed over—white disks without pupils. *Finally.*

He prepared to pull Evangeline from the water and resuscitate her before carrying her away. And then, she blinked. *Impossible.* The humming began again. *Impossible!* Her ghoulish white eyes stared right into Malledy's and a half-smile formed on her bloodless blue lips. Her hands reached up and pressed against his body.

Frozen icicles tickled Malledy's chest and then suddenly drove inside his heart like white-hot daggers. *WHAT IS GOING ON?* Malledy couldn't move to push away Evangeline's hands. He felt his racing heartbeat slow to a rhythmic thud, then miss a beat…and then another. All he could do was listen in horror to the wordless tune Evangeline hummed and silently scream as his heartbeat stuttered, skipped, and finally disappeared.

CHAPTER THIRTY-TWO

Evangeline pulled herself out of the frigid water, gasping for air, drawing a lungful through her ravaged throat. Malledy lay on the creek bank, his legs sprawled over hers, his torso and face in the dirt. He wasn't moving and it didn't look like he was breathing, either. *What just happened?* One second he'd been drowning her, even though he claimed he needed her. *To heal him?* The next second, the boy she had known as Tristin was dead and she was alive.

A sound caught her attention. Melia was still alive, struggling to breathe. Pushing Malledy's legs off hers, Evangeline struggled to her knees and crawled over to Melia. Her friend's sweater had turned black with blood and Evangeline could see where even more blood had seeped into the dirt. The air smelled like hot, copper and she gagged.

"Tristin?" Melia whispered. A rivulet of bright-red blood dribbled from the corner of her mouth and ran down her cheek.

Evangeline's wet hair rained down on Melia's chalk-white face. "I don't know what happened—he was trying to drown me and I passed out. When I woke up—" Evangeline faltered. "Melia, I'm sorry—he's dead." *But I'm not sorry, am I? He tried to kill me, so I—*

No! I've never even hit a person in my life. How could I just have killed someone?

Reaching up with bloody fingers, Melia touched a bruise already turning purple on Evangeline's cheek. "So…sorry—didn't know…" And then she began coughing uncontrollably, bloody froth coating her mouth. "You've got to…get out of…here."

"I need to get you to a hospital."

Melia shook her head.

"Melia, there's a lot of blood, okay? A lot. You need a doctor." *Please don't die on me! You're not who I thought you were, and you chose your boyfriend over me, at least for a while, but somehow I still love you.* "Life is less black and white than I thought," Evangeline said softly.

Tears streaming, Melia met Evangeline's eyes and a look of complete understanding passed between them: *I was never a kid and you can no longer be one either.* Melia nodded slightly and coughed so hard, it was agony to watch.

"Get his—gun," Melia gasped.

"What? I don't know how to use a gun!"

"Get—it!" Melia said forcefully. "Hide…it in case…Now!"

Evangeline limped over to the revolver lying beside Malledy's body. She picked it up and tied it to the front string of her pajama bottoms, tucking it inside the band and pulling her oversized flannel top over it. "I think I can carry you," she said, returning to Melia's side.

"To use…gun…flip off…safety on top…point and pull…trigger…easy-peasy," Melia said, her bloodstained lips forming a ghastly smile.

"This. Is. Really. Happening." Evangeline forced herself to accept her new reality because hiding from it might get her recaptured…or worse.

Melia's body was wracked with coughing. Evangeline scrambled for a way to help her friend.

"Melia, you said I had the power to heal Tristin—er, Malledy. Tell me how! Tell me and I'll heal you. Tell me!" Evangeline pulled Melia close. "Tell me!"

"I don't…know…how." Melia spoke so softly that Evangeline had trouble hearing her. "Remember…the… butterfly?"

Melia whimpered in pain and Evangeline gently lowered her body back to the ground.

"Would've…been easier…if I hated…you," Melia murmured. And then she sighed and her eyes became fixed on nothing.

"Please," Evangeline whispered, but Melia was dead. Evangeline wrapped her arms around her knees and huddled beside her best friend, soaked, shivering, covered in blood and dirt, and utterly alone in the world…except she wasn't alone.

Evangeline heard the two members of Pandora as they broke through the foliage.

Juliette and an older member named Dawn took in the scene, faces somber.

"Are you hurt?" Dawn asked, kneeling beside Evangeline, checking her body for wounds.

"No. But Melia's hurt," Evangeline said. "I think she's… dead."

Dawn checked Melia's limp wrist for a pulse. "Yes. She's dead—serves her right."

"What?! How can you say that? She was one of you!"

"She was a traitor. If that kid hadn't killed her, we would've."

"I'll dispose of the bodies," Juliette said. "You get Evangeline back to the safe house. Where's the gun?"

"He threw it into the bushes," Evangeline said, lying so smoothly she would've been shocked if she wasn't so numb.

"Holy Gods!" Dawn gasped, thankfully distracted from Evangeline's lie. She'd just seen the golden box resting beneath some brush. "Is that it?" she called over to Juliette.

Juliette looked over her shoulder to the spot where Dawn was pointing. "*Oui*. Quickly now! Take it and go! I'll find the gun after I'm done with them."

Very gently, Dawn picked up the box, cradling it almost, and placed it in Melia's backpack.

"Can you walk?" she asked Evangeline.

Evangeline didn't answer. Taking off her own sneakers and socks, Dawn fitted them onto Evangeline's feet.

"Let's get you out of here," she said, tying the laces.

Evangeline tried not to look at Melia's body, but she couldn't help it. Her best friend was dead—shot in the stomach. It didn't matter to Evangeline who Tristin or Malledy had really been. All that mattered was that Melia was gone. *Dead.* No matter what she'd done, in the end, Melia had stepped in to take the bullet and save Evangeline. Whether she'd done it out of friendship or duty, Evangeline would never know. *Does it really matter?*

"Melia saved my life," Evangeline said, but if Dawn heard her, she didn't let on.

They walked past Juliette kneeling beside Malledy's body, one hand resting on his chest.

"Juliette, call Samantha. Tell her the threat has been neutralized, that I have the descendant, and we're on the way back."

"*Oui*," Juliette said. "*D'accord.*"

Samantha. Evangeline felt the revolver she'd hidden against her stomach. It was time to face her godmother once and for all. It was time to get some answers. She wondered if she'd die tonight, too, and realized that she no longer really cared because she'd rather be dead than live as a prisoner for the rest of her days. *Ready or not, Samantha, here I come.*

CHAPTER THIRTY-THREE

"Where are we really going Raphe?"

"My house."

Dr. Sullivan pulled over to the side of the road and cut the engine. He flipped over Raphe's right hand, pointing to an address scribbled on his palm.

"Look, you don't strike me as mentally challenged, so I'm going to make a leap and deduct that you don't need to write your own address down on your hand."

Raphe ran his other hand through his wet hair, stalling. "Okay, okay. You're driving me to my teacher's house."

"And why's that?"

Raphe was silent.

"Kid, in two seconds I'm going to turn this car around, go back to the hospital, and tell Detective Morrison everything you just told me, even though I'm not sure I believe any of it."

Raphe met Dr. Sullivan's angry gaze. "I think my teacher, Mrs. Hopkins, knows where Samantha Harris is. If I can find Sam, then I can find Evangeline and save her."

Dr. Sullivan turned the ignition key and the car purred back to life. He put his blinker on and made a U-turn.

"Stop, please!" Raphe begged. Come on! Evangeline thinks *I'm* part of everything that's happened to her today! She saw a picture of my mother in Samantha's apartment and she totally freaked. I'd never do anything to hurt her and I need her to know that! That's why I've got to find her. Please!"

Dr. Sullivan kept driving.

"Look at it this way, if you help me, and I find Evangeline, she'll be safe and you'll be out of the equation. Then you can keep drinking until you forget your wife and daughter ever existed, just like my dad forgot about us."

Dr. Sullivan slowed the car, looked at Raphe for a long moment, and then made another U-turn.

CHAPTER THIRTY-FOUR

Evangeline ran the delicate chain through her fingers, searching for the clasp. She went around once, twice, three times. But there was no clasp.

"It won't reappear," Samantha explained, "until you give the necklace to your own daughter on her sixteenth birthday."

Evangeline hadn't heard her godmother enter the room. "So, you finally found the time to visit me in my prison?" Evangeline hoped her voice was dripping with enough sarcasm.

She had washed off Melia's blood and Dawn had bandaged her feet and then left her alone to "get some rest." Instead, Evangeline had changed into her original hoodie and jeans, which had been washed, neatly folded, and placed in a dresser drawer. She'd tucked Malledy's gun into her waistband, hidden beneath her oversized top.

"At least you're talking to me," Sam said, pulling the desk chair beside the bed on which Evangeline sat cross-legged. Her godmother was wearing an ivory-colored sweater and green corduroys. Evangeline had never seen her dressed so casually. There were dark-gray circles beneath her eyes. *Good—she's exhausted, too.*

"Why did you try to kill my mom?"

Samantha paled and Evangeline was happy to see she'd hurt her.

"I tried to tell you at the hospital, but there wasn't enough time to explain. I did it for Olivia—for your mom and for you."

"Liar!"

Sam recoiled at Evangeline's fury. "Don't use that tone with me, young lady."

"Oh, get off it. I'm not a young lady anymore. You and your friends have made sure of that. And you've lost the right to tell me what's appropriate for me to do."

Samantha look pained. "Evangeline, I prayed that Olivia's death would be quick. But the Gods are cruel and chose otherwise, so I tried to help your mother die with some dignity."

"*Dignity* was a pillow over her face from the person she thought was her best friend?"

"She deserved better, I know," Sam said, leaning forward, her forehead furrowed, eyes glistening. "Don't you think I know that? E, your mother was like a little sister to me—I loved her more than anyone in this world, but I couldn't save her—no one could. Ending Olivia's life as painlessly as possible was the only choice in my power. She was cursed by Zeus and she was going to die, just as the descendants before her always died—violently, painfully, and without nobility. I'm not proud of what I did, but I would do it again for Olivia's sake."

"Spare me your rationale for attempted murder," Evangeline said in disgust. "How long have you been in this cult?"

"It's a Sect." Samantha leaned back in her chair. "I've been a part of it since I was twelve-years-old. My mother was a member of Pandora, and her mother before her going back for a very long time. And now I'm the Sect Leader."

"Good for you," Evangeline said, clapping in slow motion. "You must be so proud. You've done a great job. Let's see, you've lied to my mom and me our whole lives without us figuring it out. You must've felt very smart and thought we were pretty dumb, huh?"

"Evangeline—"

"No, we should go through all your big accomplishments as leader of Pandora, Sam." Evangeline felt her cheeks flush and her temper flare. "You tried to kill my mom when she got sick and needed you the most. That was particularly impressive. You drugged and kidnapped me and locked me in a prison. You should be really proud, especially since all my favorite things are in here. Nice."

"Are you through?

Evangeline felt sick to her stomach. She wanted to make Sam hurt like she did, or hide beneath the quilt, go to sleep and forget everything. Neither was an option. "What's your real name?"

"Samantha Nedrow."

"Do you know that Melia's *dead*? Dead, like a hole in her stomach and blood everywhere. Dead like never coming back." Evangeline's insides felt raw and she could barely swallow the thick lump in her throat. *I'm never going to see Melia again. She's been my best friend since we were little. She saved my life. Now she's the first person I loved to die. Will she be the last?*

"Melia was sixteen, Sam. But she was a *traitor*, right? So you would've killed her anyway? Good riddance. Again, fantastic job, clearly you've inspired great loyalty in your followers."

"Enough," Sam said. Her hands were casually folded in her lap, but the knuckles were white.

Evangeline took a deep breath. She needed to be calm if she was going to get out of this place. "Is my mother still alive?"

"Yes—but she has congestive heart failure and her organs are shutting down one by one. E, I know it's hard for you to comprehend all of this—"

"Because it's insane."

"For your sake, I truly wish that it was." Sam blinked back tears.

Crocodile tears. "Don't bother crying. It won't make me believe you or forgive you for what you've done." Evangeline looked around the room. "So, this is it? Your big plan is to keep me locked up in this room until I magically produce the next descendant?"

Samantha stood up. "My *big plan*, as you call it, was to never have you find out who you really are. My big plan was to protect you, just as I protected Olivia, so that you could live a normal life. But once you saw me in the hospital and found my apartment, it was too late. I know you as if you were my own child, Evangeline. You would never have let what you saw go." Samantha walked toward the door. "In time, you'll come to understand who you are and accept your fate. Then I can give you back your freedom."

Freedom? That's a lie. "I'll never be free again."

"Not like before, no," Sam agreed, "but that life you were living was just an illusion."

"You really believe it all?" Evangeline asked, a feeling of overwhelming exasperation almost choking her. "Pandora, the box, descendants, gifts from the Gods? You believe that I can sing because Apollo decreed it, and kill because Athena gave me that gift? You actually think that Hephaestus gave me the power to create reality from my own imagination? For God's sake, Sam, you believe that I can grow and heal things because Demeter bestowed that gift on a mythical woman named Pandora who only ever lived in Greek mythology?"

Samantha's eyes met Evangeline's. "Maybe you don't have all the gifts the Gods bequeathed—through the centuries, some are lost to the descendants as their genes are mixed with mere mortals. Sometimes, if those gifts do appear, they are weaker than the Gods originally decreed and descendants can only marginally control them. But one thing always happens. When a descendant turns sixteen and puts on the key necklace she becomes beautiful. I can't explain why, but this metamorphosis has happened without fail throughout Pandora's history."

"I don't believe anything you're saying."

"Look back on your life, Evangeline—on you mom's life. Think about all the things you could never quite explain— all the inconsistencies that made you feel different—all the strange occurrences and abilities. And then ask yourself, how can you not believe?"

"Because I'm not crazy!"

"Dawn said Melia's boyfriend tried to drown you."

Evangeline's heart skipped a beat. She looked away from her godmother.

"How long did he hold your head beneath the water?"

"I don't know. A while. I can't remember."

Samantha arched an eyebrow. "Poseidon decreed that Pandora and her descendants would never drown. And don't forget, you killed that boy. Athena would be proud."

Evangeline felt a chill blanket her entire body. *I couldn't have killed Tristin...could I?* But before she could reply to

Samantha's ridiculous statements or pull out the revolver, her godmother had slipped out the door and the locks were again thrown into place.

"I. Am. Not. The. Descendant. Of. Pandora!" Evangeline screamed. "I am not!" *Please—please—please don't let this be true...*

CHAPTER THIRTY-FIVE

They drove by a cedar house set on a one-lane road. The name on the mailbox was M. Hopkins. There were no other houses on the desolate street. Raphe insisted that Dr. Sullivan park a half-mile away and then bushwhack through dense woods so that they could approach Mrs. Hopkins' home from the rear.

"Maybe I *am* drunk," Dr. Sullivan grumbled. "Tell me again, what do you plan to do once we get to the house?"

"Find out if Evangeline is inside," Raphe whispered.

"Okay. How?

"Look in the windows."

"So, we'll get arrested for being Peeping Toms," Dr. Sullivan muttered. "And then?"

"Sneak in and get her out of there."

Dr. Sullivan grabbed Raphe's arm. "Whoa there double-o-seven."

"Shhh!"

Dr. Sullivan lowered his voice. "I told you, Raphe, we're not breaking and entering. We agreed that if I drove you here, and confirmed that Evangeline was in the house, we'd call the police."

"But if we have the chance to get her out—"

"No."

"You could've just dropped me off."

"Yeah, that would've been a responsible move."

Raphe looked down at his sneakers. "If we call the cops my mom will go to jail."

"If you really saw your mom helping kidnap Evangeline, then she deserves to go to jail."

Raphe sighed. "Okay—okay—you win."

He shook free of Dr. Sullivan and they pushed through a thick clump of briars. Glimpsing a building through the foliage, they crept forward. It was a greenhouse. They approached it cautiously, catching sight of the Hopkins' house only twenty-five feet in front of it.

A light from the second floor blinked on. Instinctively, Raphe and Dr. Sullivan crouched behind a tree. Even from such a distance, they could make out a figure walking past the illuminated window, then turning and pressing their hands against the glass, staring out into the night. It was Evangeline.

Raphe leapt to his feet and bolted toward the house.

"Damn!" Dr. Sullivan ran after the kid.

CHAPTER THIRTY-SIX

Evangeline moved away from the bathroom window—there was no escape that way. She splashed cold water on her face. The bruise on her cheek was purple and her lower lip was crusted with dried blood.

"Who are you?" she whispered. But the girl reflected back was a stranger and only the black key responded—glinting in the light with a conspiratorial wink. *What did it matter, anyway?* Whether she was the fantasy descendant that Samantha and Melia believed in, or just a kid whose mom was dying and who'd been kidnapped by a cult, she was still standing in this bathroom with a guard waiting outside the door to lock her up again.

Drawing Malledy's revolver from where it was tucked against the small of her back, Evangeline looked for the safety. She flipped it off, just as Melia had instructed. *"Point and pull the trigger easy-peasy."* But was it that easy to kill someone?

There's no other way out of this place, Evangeline told herself. And the longer she waited, the harder it'd be. *Can I pull the trigger?* "I guess we'll find out," Evangeline said to the bruised and battered girl staring at her from the mirror. And then she opened the door.

CHAPTER THIRTY-SEVEN

Raphe was well inside the house before Dr. Sullivan had stepped through the back door into a mudroom filled with coats, boot, and shoes of various sizes. The light was murky, but the doctor could just see Raphe as he crept into a large, empty kitchen. There was nothing he could do but follow, wincing as he stepped on a creaky floorboard.

Glancing over his shoulder, Raphe held a finger to his lips. Then he turned and walked beneath the arch leading into the front hall. There was a room to the left and a curved, wooden staircase to the right. Raphe was starting to climb the stairs when the doctor caught up to him, reaching for his shoulder.

And then the entire room was suddenly flooded with light.

"Welcome to my home," Melodie Hopkins said from a seat in the living room.

Raphe and the doctor whirled around to see fifteen women sitting calmly on an assortment of velvet chairs and floral sofas. There was a collection of guns, knives, and tasers among the group.

"I know Raphe from school, of course, but who's this man?" Melodie asked.

"He was Olivia's doctor," Samantha said, gesturing toward a couch. "Please, Dr. Sullivan, come in and sit down."

"I'm *still* her doctor," Dr. Sullivan said, not making a move toward the couch. "She's not dead yet—no thanks to you."

"Semantics," Sam replied.

"Mom?" Raphe was staring wide-eyed at a woman who stood beside a large picture window.

"I can't help you, Raphe," Beca Petersen said to her son, her voice heavy with emotion. "No one can help you now."

"You're right, kid, she *is* a heartless witch," Dr. Sullivan put an arm around Raphe's shoulders. "We'll be going now." He turned Raphe around and began walking out of the room.

"One more step," Samantha warned, "and you're both dead."

CHAPTER THIRTY-EIGHT

Evangeline walked out of the bathroom. "That was quick," Stephanie said. "After you." She gestured down the hall toward Evangeline's room.

"No," Evangeline raised the revolver. "After you."

Stephanie's gasped, deep-set eyes widening. "You don't want to do this, Evangeline. You're a sweet girl, not a killer."

I was, but your freakish cult killed that girl; Malledy killed her; Melia's death killed her.

"Turn around and go." Evangeline pressed the revolver into Stephanie's back.

The woman turned and walked down the hallway. "You'll never get past them all."

"Shut up!" *I'm terrified enough without you talking.*

They descended the steps one by one. Each time Stephanie hesitated, Evangeline jammed the gun harder into her spine.

Am I really doing this? There was light filtering from the first floor hall and Evangeline hoped that it'd been left on by accident and that all the freaks were safely asleep and out of the way. They descended the final steps. Peering into the front hall and living room beyond, Evangeline saw that she couldn't have been more wrong.

"She's got a gun!" Stephanie called.

Evangeline took in the faces staring at her. There were at least a dozen Sect members in the living room, including Samantha, Mrs. Hopkins, that Goth Girl, Lacie, and Raphe's mom. *Who isn't in this cult?* Some of them had guns. Evangeline's breath caught in her throat when she saw Dr. Sullivan. "What're *you* doing here?"

Dr. Sullivan looked up from the couch, his glasses slightly askew. "I keep asking myself that same question." He nodded toward Raphe. "He brought me."

Evangeline looked at Raphe, who appeared confused, scared. *Nice act.*

"How can she have a gun?" Samantha demanded, face flushed, tone furious. "Where the hell is Juliette?"

"Still burying the bodies," Dawn replied. "Evangeline lied—she told us the boy threw his gun into the woods. She must've hidden it—"

"Really?" Samantha snapped. "You think so?"

"She's talking about Melia and Tristin," Evangeline peered at Raphe, feeling her anger spark, ignite, and then burn bright. "Melia's *dead* and it's *your* fault! Do you get that?

And," she nodded at Dr. Sullivan, "how could you involve him in all of this?"

"E, you've got it all wrong," Raphe said, trying to stand up. Roughly, Dawn pushed him back down. "I didn't know. When I saw that picture in Sammy's loft, I was as shocked as you were. I got Dr. Sullivan to drive me here because Mrs. Hopkins was in the photo. I thought she'd know where you were—*Melia's dead*? I can't believe it!" He reached for his inhaler, but Dawn grabbed his wrist.

Evangeline rounded on Samantha, her anger a living, breathing creature that was giving her courage. "Is this all part of your plan, too? Get me to trust Raphe again? Fool me once." She edged the revolver up from Stephanie's back to her temple.

"You can believe whatever you want," Samantha said. "But put down that gun!"

"Athena gave me the strength to kill," Evangeline reminded her godmother. She tightened her index finger against the trigger. "Don't make me show you how well I can do it. Let Dr. Sullivan and me walk out of this house, and I'll let Stephanie go."

Samantha stood up. "Stephanie and every member of Pandora pledged to protect the descendant and the artifacts with their lives. If Stephanie has to die, that's acceptable."

Goth Girl took a few steps toward Evangeline. "Don't you understand that Tristin wasn't the first to try to kill you?"

"Because I'm so special, Lacie, is that it?" Evangeline snapped.

"Yes, that's right," Lacie replied without hesitation.

"Whether you accept it or not," Samantha said, "you're Pandora's descendant, Evangeline."

"I don't know what the hell is going on here!" Dr. Sullivan held up his hands. "But it's gone too far."

"You're right," Samantha agreed and nodded toward Melodie Hopkins, who immediately raised her pistol, aiming it at Dr. Sullivan's chest.

Outside the house, someone was watching the drama unfold, and waiting for just the right moment...

CHAPTER THIRTY-NINE

"No!" Evangeline shouted. "Leave him alone, he's not part of this!"

"Your dear Dr. Sullivan knows too much," Melodie responded. The doctor just sat there. He seemed to be in shock.

There's only one thing I can do to save him. Quick as lightning, Evangeline shoved Stephanie hard, sending her stumbling across the hallway floor. She quickly turned the revolver on herself, pressing it into her stomach.

"I'll kill myself," she said in a steady voice. "If you hurt Dr. Sullivan, I'll pull the trigger. I swear it."

"Put that gun down!" Melodie demanded.

"We're not in school anymore," Evangeline replied. "You're not my teacher here. If you don't let Dr. Sullivan go right now, Sam, I'll do it." *Am I really doing this?*

"Don't!" Dr. Sullivan stared at Evangeline, horrified. "For what it's worth, I don't think Raphe knew anything about whatever it is that's going on here!"

Evangeline's hands were slippery with sweat. *There's no way out of this. If I live, Dr. Sullivan dies. If I die, Dr. Sullivan dies, and if he's right about Raphe, my friend dies, too. If I live, both of their deaths will be my fault. If I live, I'm never getting out of here.* Evangeline began to press the trigger—

A single gunshot rang out.

Instantly, a barrage of gunfire volleyed, filling the room with smoke and the stench of burned gunpowder. Seconds later, two people lay on the floor bleeding out from their wounds.

Someone screamed.

CHAPTER FORTY

"Who the hell is he?" Samantha demanded, looking down at a young man in a shiny leather jacket writhing on the floor, his slick purple intestines spilling out of the bloody gash in his stomach.

Stephanie crouched beside the man, a blood-covered blade in her right hand. "Not sure, but I think I've cut him too deeply to get any answers from him now."

"I know him." Lacie said in a flat voice. "He told me his name was Ivan. I met him at a coffee shop on 23rd Street. We were dating." Ivan moaned. A few seconds later, he was dead.

Evangeline tried to yell, but even though her mouth was moving, no words came out. Only moments ago a man had burst through the front door, gun in hand. And then a body was racing across the living room, rocketing through the hall and launching into the air. Raphe. He'd seen the man running toward Evangeline—he'd burst off the couch, sprinted, and then dove between them. Now Raphe lay sprawled with blood saturating his T-shirt and staining the beige carpet beneath his still body. His head was turned sideways, awkwardly, eyes closed, hair tousled like he'd just stepped off his skateboard. *Raphe just saved my life. He really didn't know about any of this! He's going to die because of me, too.*

"Help," Evangeline whispered, looking desperately at Dr. Sullivan, who was still on the couch. His glasses were gone, but he hadn't been hurt—he was just frozen in place.

"Dr. Sullivan," Evangeline said softly, "please help. HELP!" Her scream managed to wake the doctor, who tried to stand up. One of the women shoved him back onto the couch.

"Dammit, I'm a doctor! Let me help the boy!"

"Let him," Samantha said, glancing over at Beca. Raphe's mother stood motionless, her face as white as a ghost's.

Dr. Sullivan rushed to kneel beside Raphe. He pulled up the T-shirt. There was a bullet hole in his lower abdomen.

"Help me roll him," Dr. Sullivan commanded. No one moved. "Evangeline, help me."

Evangeline put down the revolver and joined the doctor. They rolled Raphe onto his side and Dr. Sullivan wiped away the blood on the boy's back so he could see more clearly. There were two bullet holes in Raphe's back.

"One bullet is still inside. We need to get him to the hospital. There isn't time to call an ambulance—we've got to drive there ourselves. Now!"

"No," Samantha said. "Try to make him comfortable—
that's all we can do for him now."

"How do you expect me to do that?" Dr. Sullivan lashed
out. "I took an oath to save lives. That's what I do."

Samantha didn't reply.

"Look, lady, there's no telling the amount of damage that's
been done to Raphe's bowels, colon, kidney, or liver, but this
is a lethal injury. He needs to be rushed into an OR where
surgeons will have to open him up and attempt to suture
myriad organs that may or may not be vital enough to save.
This is no longer some little sorority game—"

"You think that's what this is?" Beca Petersen shouted.
"You think I'd let my son die for a game?!" She was spraying
spit with every word. "This is as real as it gets!"

Stephanie slapped Beca, her palm leaving a bloody smear
across Beca's cheek. Raphe's mother slumped onto a couch,
sobbing and moaning. Stephanie sat down beside her, an arm
around her shaking shoulders.

"Let Dr. Sullivan take him to the hospital," Evangeline
begged her godmother.

Samantha shook her head.

"He won't tell on you," Evangeline said, looking at Dr.
Sullivan. "Right? You won't tell, right?"

"Of course he will," Samantha said. "He's the kind of man
who'd have to tell."

Dr. Sullivan's hands were covered with blood, his face
grim. "So what now? We all watch this innocent boy die and

then I'm next? At least have the decency to make Evangeline leave the room when you shoot me."

"No," Evangeline said, tears running down her cheeks. "No—no—no!" She pressed her hands against the wound on Raphe's stomach, trying to staunch the blood. *There's too much.*

"You're all hypocrites!" she shouted. "You say you exist to protect the world—to protect living, breathing people from Annihilation—but you'd throw away Raphe's life without a second thought!"

"And you'd rather kill yourself than believe," Melodie fired back.

"I'm sixteen! I have my whole life ahead of me. I have plans that don't include your voodoo magic and people that want to kill me!" Evangeline's head was throbbing. "I want to have a boyfriend—go to college—figure out a career—eventually get married—have kids—live until I'm an old woman! I don't want the freaking job you nut-bags keep trying to shove down my throat!"

She pressed her hands harder against Raphe's wound, but the blood was gushing out, hot, slippery, and endless.

"Dr. Sullivan?" She looked at him.

"It's no use, Evangeline." The doctor sounded defeated. "Better to let the blood flow, so the poor thing can die quickly. I'm so sorry."

"Evangeline was ready to shoot herself," Lacie pronounced. "How can she possibly protect the box when she doesn't even care about her own life?"

Evangeline glared at her classmate. "Go to hell, Lacie. I care about things that are real."

"You are the only person standing between mankind and Annihilation," Samantha said.

"F-you!"

"Is that the best you can do?"

"What do you want from me?" Evangeline half-shouted, half-moaned.

"Everything," Samantha replied. "There's more to Pandora's history—an addition to Zeus' Curse. It was so devastating that the first members of Pandora decreed that it should never be written down. Instead it's been passed solely by word of mouth from leader to leader. Evangeline, if you die before having a daughter, then anyone can take the key you wear and open Pandora's Box. All they have to do is kill you."

"For God's sake, give the kid a break," Dr. Sullivan said, utterly revolted.

Samantha met the doctor's eyes. "Evangeline is the only impediment the Gods gave us to provide a degree of separation from the devastation of Annihilation. It's not much, I admit that, but it's all we've had for thousands of years. And Pandora has sacrificed countless women to make it enough."

"E?" Raphe's voice was so quiet that she almost didn't hear him.

Raphe's eyes fluttered open and Evangeline tried to smile at him. "Raphe, we're going to get you to the hospital. It's going to be okay."

He struggled to breathe and began to cough. Evangeline pulled him onto her lap so that his head was raised. "I didn't... know...any of...it."

"I know that now," Evangeline said, trying to sound strong. "I'm sorry I ever thought that you were part of this. I should've trusted you."

"S'okay." Raphe winced and a moan escaped his lips. "Hurts, burns...a ton...was going to ask you...prom."

"Yes," Evangeline said. "I'll go to prom with you. But first we have to get you fixed up."

She knew she was crying, but she couldn't stop and her tears fell onto Raphe's face, mingling with his own. The intensity of Raphe's golden-brown eyes seemed to be fading and his breathing sounded just like Melia's had—wet, hitching, temporary.

"Don't try to talk," Evangeline said. "Everything's going to be okay. I'm okay—you saved me—and you'll be okay, too."

And then she started to hum—the tune that was always floating somewhere in her mind. She wasn't sure why she was doing it, but maybe it could somehow help Raphe find peace—the way her mom's singing had always soothed her.

Find peace, Raphe—let me give you this last gift. Her hands were still pressed against Raphe's abdomen, feeling the hot blood, the battered skin, the ragged hole. Her fingers started tingling and then began to throb. She didn't withdraw them, instead closing her eyes and relishing the pain because she deserved it. All of this was her fault.

The torment intensified. Evangeline's hands felt like they'd been doused in gasoline and ignited, enveloped by flame, searing and charring, the agony seeping like boiling oil into her bones—red and white torture that burned, flared, and swallowed her whole.

Raphe drew his final breath.

Chapter Forty-one

Evangeline felt the flow of blood slow and then stop under her fingers. The heat in her hands dissipated, leaving only a shadow of the sensation that had moments ago enveloped her entire body. She felt horribly empty and the key was suddenly a sliver of sharp ice against her skin—as if it had been drained of all its strange energy. Her hands rested lightly on Raphe's dead body. Dr. Sullivan would soon follow her friend. There was nothing she could do to help either of them. She was powerless to fight Pandora. She'd had her chance, but in the end, she couldn't pull the trigger. *I am the passive girl the cult thought I was—I was only pretending to be strong and brave. I'm as much of a hypocrite as they are.*

"And the Goddess Demeter gave Pandora the power to make anything grow and heal," Samantha said softly.

"E?"

Evangeline felt her heart leap and crash against her chest. She opened her eyes to see Raphe gazing up at her, his eyes a vibrant amber, a tinge of pink returning to his cheeks. *How?*

"Remember the butterfly," Melia had whispered before she'd died.

I healed that yellow butterfly with a torn wing by humming a song I've always somehow known. I hummed that same song with Raphe...

Evangeline stared at Raphe's stomach—the ragged hole was now a shiny pink welt and the skin around it was fading from a deep purple to a pale-blue ringed with shades of yellow. Evangeline stared at her hands. One was closed into a fist. Slowly she opened it—a bullet rested in her palm. *What is going on?!*

"What happened," Raphe asked, looking at Dr. Sullivan, who was staring wide-eyed at Evangeline. "Doc, did you save my life?"

The doctor shook his head. "I think *she* did, kid," he said, nodding at Evangeline. "I don't know how...but she did."

Evangeline offered the bullet to Samantha, who approached silently. As the bullet slid from her palm into Sam's outstretched hand, a great sense of letting go washed over her. *I don't believe it all—how can I? But something inexplicable just happened. I need to stop fighting and try to understand.*

Evangeline met Sam's eyes. "I don't get any of this—not really. It's too much with my mom and my friends and—it's just too much all at once for me to make any sense of. But one thing seems clear. Whatever happened—is happening—will happen—it's not just up to you anymore. Both Dr. Sullivan and Raphe would've died for me, too. Let them live. Please."

Samantha weighed Evangeline's words. "We've never allowed outsiders who know about a descendant, the box, and the key to live. It's too much of a risk."

"Sam, I know now that I can't just walk away from Pandora," Evangeline replied, stunned by her own calm and sincerity. "Even if you couldn't find me, the people you're all sworn to protect me from eventually would. I don't believe what either faction believes, but I do understand that you'll both do anything to achieve your goals. I do get that, okay?"

Samantha nodded.

"So, somehow the Sect and I need to work together to make my life worth living or, if what you believe about Pandora's Box and my enemies is true, none of us will ever survive."

Samantha studied Raphe, Dr. Sullivan and Evangeline, her lips pressed into a tight white line. Time seemed to slow as three lives hung in the balance…

Chapter Forty-two

Juliette entered the mudroom. She heard voices in the living room, but didn't approach. She opened a narrow door set against the far wall of the kitchen and climbed the back staircase to the second floor. She walked down to the last door on the right and slipped into the sewing room.

Melia's backpack rested against a bolt of red velvet leaning on wooden shelves overflowing with needles, thread, and quilting squares of every imaginable color and pattern. She rifled through the backpack and withdrew Pandora's Box. She placed it carefully in the bottom of the purse.

She left the second floor by way of the same staircase and slid into the dark night without detection. Before entering the woods, she glanced back at the house. Pandora had been her pre-ordained fate, but it was not to be her destiny.

CHAPTER FORTY-THREE

"You still want to kill me, don't you?" Dr. Sullivan asked.

Melodie Hopkins regarded him from behind her enormous glasses. "It's not my decision to make. Samantha is our leader, and she decreed that you and Raphe live—but we'll be watching you very closely."

Melodie had allowed Dr. Sullivan, Raphe and Evangeline to stop by the doctor's house to shower and put on clean clothes. Evangeline had scrubbed the blood off until her arms and face were raw, and put on some jeans and a sweater that had once belonged to the doctor's wife. Dr. Sullivan also gave Raphe one of his Middlebury sweatshirts and a pair of khakis one size too big.

Melodie drove them to the hospital where they'd met Samantha. Dr. Sullivan hadn't recognized Evangeline's godmother in an auburn wig and blue contact lenses, but Evangeline had walked right up to her.

"Let's do this," she'd said, and they'd followed Evangeline to her mother's room where the first rays of morning were just beginning to filter through the window.

"Dr. Sullivan, are you letting Evangeline do this because you believe in all we've said?" Samantha asked quietly from the corner of the room.

"Belief is a process," Dr. Sullivan replied.

The three adults paused to watch Evangeline drag a chair next to the bed.

"Will this really work?" Melodie asked.

"Olivia is in the final stage of congestive heart failure," Dr. Sullivan said. Both her kidneys are shot, and she's unable to breathe on her own. There's probably brain damage, too. It would take a miracle."

"She deserves the chance to try," Samantha said.

"Yes," Dr. Sullivan nodded. "We can agree on that."

"Can we also agree that the drinking has to stop?" Sam asked. The doctor's face reddened.

"How can you even *consider* this man as an appropriate guardian?" Melodie asked Samantha, glaring at Dr. Sullivan.

"Look, it can't be me. Better the devil we know—and it's what she wants."

"Why are you willing to take on such an enormous responsibility?" Melodie demanded of the doctor.

He took off his glasses and cleaned them methodically with the corner of his shirt. "My dad died of cancer when I was seven and my mom was killed by a drunk driver a few years later. I spent the next eight years in foster care. I'm willing to take the responsibility because when I was Evangeline's age no one helped me." Dr. Sullivan put his glasses back on. "And because I have no family of my own left to care about."

Melodie considered Dr. Sullivan's unflinching eyes and the blush coloring his cheeks. "Okay," she said finally.

By this time, Evangeline was seated beside the bed holding her mother's right hand, trying to shut out the odor of chemicals, disinfectant, and sickness and the raised whispers of the adults behind her. The woman in the bed didn't look anything like her mom, but Evangeline could somehow feel her mom trapped inside the swollen body.

Tell me what to do, she silently prayed. *Please tell me.* She tightened her grip and suddenly her mom squeezed her hand back.

Evangeline gasped, closed her eyes and then opened them. Her mom was gazing right at her. There were no tubes or IV lines attached. Her mother was radiant once more—blue eyes clear and pain-free, hair shining, body returned to its original, petite, perfect size.

The woman smiled at her daughter. "Quite a few days you've had, my girl."

Evangeline forced herself to remain calm. She didn't know how long this would last and she didn't want to waste a second. "Mom, tell me how to help you!"

Her mother raised her daughter's hand and kissed it. "You already know. I love you, honey."

A lump caught in Evangeline's throat. "I love you, too."

"I know. No matter what happens next, I'll always be with you. I'm proud of you, E."

And then, her mother's beautiful face slowly morphed back into reality and she was once again hooked to a ventilator and countless other machines, imprisoned in a bloated body that was no longer her own.

"Did you see that? Did you see, Raphe?" Evangeline looked over at Raphe, who was sitting on the windowsill. He looked beyond pale and totally exhausted, but no longer half-dead. Raphe shook his head. Evangeline wiped her eyes. *You already know.* Then why am I so terrified? She knew the answer. *I'm afraid to let her go because I want to keep my mom with me no matter what.*

Evangeline thought about the miserable-looking patients wandering the hospital corridors hooked to their IVs, being pumped full of fluids and drugs. Dr. Sullivan had said that those drugs couldn't help her mother; that they'd only prolong her misery. *I already know.*

"I want to unplug the ventilator."

Dr. Sullivan walked over to the bed. "Evangeline, that's your right as her only family, but you do understand that it's the only thing keeping your mother alive now, don't you?"

Evangeline nodded, her eyes fixed on her mother's face. "I understand that you believe that and a big part of me does, too. But what about what happened with Raphe?"

"I can't explain what you did," Dr. Sullivan admitted.

"If this doesn't work—if I can't help my mom begin to heal…then maybe it's—maybe it's kinder to let her go."

Dr. Sullivan nodded.

She kissed her mother's cheek. "I love you, mom."

Evangeline began to hum the sweet, haunting melody and placed one hand over her mom's heart and the other on her forehead. Her fingertips responded instantly—tingling, the pressure increasing, building, throbbing, heat coursing through her palms. Closing her eyes, she let the pain multiply upon itself until it thundered and roiled through her body.

"Dr. Sullivan, turn it off," Evangeline gasped. "Now!" And then Evangeline abandoned herself to the wildfire.

CHAPTER FORTY-FOUR

The heart-rate monitor showed a steady, flat neon-green line, making a dull, monotone sound that echoed sharply in the room. It remained that way for several minutes until finally Dr. Sullivan said, "I'm sorry, Evangeline, it's over." The room was heavy with silence.

"I'm so sorry, E," Raphe said, his face pinched and miserable.

Samantha walked to Evangeline's side and put a hand on her shoulder. Evangeline didn't shrug it off—she could hardly even feel it. Her body was an empty husk, burned out by the magic that had scorched her but utterly failed to save her mom's life. *So stupid. Just because I healed a butterfly and then Raphe, doesn't mean I'm capable of saving my dying mother. Who do I think I am, anyway?*

"You tried," Dr. Sullivan said. He reached up to turn off the monitor, but at the moment it beeped and the flat line on the screen formed a small peak, and then another one, and another, until the line settled into a rhythm. Olivia Theopolis was breathing. She was breathing on her own. Dr. Sullivan stared down at his patient and then over at Evangeline, at a complete loss for words.

Stacy walked into the room carrying medical supplies. She almost dropped them when she saw Evangeline and Dr. Sullivan in the room. "Jeez—you scared me. Visiting hours—"

"I told her it was okay to visit early," Dr. Sullivan interrupted.

Stacy glanced at the other people in the room. "They're from Social Services and the kid is her friend," Dr. Sullivan said quickly.

"Oh, okay. Holy crap—the ventilator!" Stacy rushed to the bed. "It's been turned off!" Stacy looked at Dr. Sullivan in confusion.

"Evangeline opted to shut off her mother's life support."

"She's breathing on her own! Look!" Grinning, Evangeline kissed her mother and then leapt up to hug Stacy. "Thanks for taking such great care of my mom."

"But...how?" Stacy asked, completely floored.

"Medicine is ninety percent science and ten percent mystery," Dr. Sullivan said solemnly. "It's nice to be surprised once in a while, isn't it?" He turned back to Evangeline. "You realize this doesn't mean—"

"I understand," Evangeline interrupted. "It's just a start."

But it *did* mean something. If what Samantha and her Pandora women believed was actually true, then Zeus' Curse could be fought. The descendants of Pandora didn't have to die in the prime of their lives. Evangeline looked at her mother breathing on her own. *Am I starting to accept it all? Can I really believe in sects and curses and gifts from the Gods? I don't know...*

Suddenly the room felt too small, the air too warm, the eyes watching her too intrusive. "I need to get some air." Evangeline walked to the door. "Stay with my mom, okay?"

"One of us should go with you," Samantha said.

"I'll go," Raphe offered, slipping off the windowsill.

"No," Evangeline said, holding up her hands. "I really need to be alone for a few minutes, okay? I'm just going to walk around the block to get some air. Please."

Samantha nodded, but she didn't look happy about it.

Evangeline walked down the hallway, her sneakers squeaking on the linoleum. The hallway clock read 6:32 AM and she wondered how many hours had passed since she'd last slept. It felt like forever. She pressed the elevator button and a car opened. It was empty. Once the doors closed, she felt an immense rush of relief. She was finally completely alone.

"What am I?" Evangeline asked the empty space. *Do I have one foot on the steps to Mount Olympus and the other in the mortal world?* She pressed the "Lobby" button and the elevator descended.

When the doors opened, a woman wearing a headscarf and over-sized sunglasses and a young man with a square of gauze taped to his cheek and wearing a green University of Oregon baseball cap stepped in.

"*Pardonez-moi*," the woman said, side-stepping Evangeline.

"That's okay," Evangeline said. The young guy stood right in her way and by the time they were done jostling to get around each other, the elevator doors had closed.

"Shoot—that was my stop."

"No, it wasn't," the guy said, looking up at Evangeline from beneath the brim of his cap.

The woman pushed the Emergency Stop button.

It's not possible. He's dead! "Tristin?"

"I told you, my name is Malledy," Malledy replied with a smile.

CHAPTER FORTY-FIVE

Evangeline wasn't screaming in the halted elevator. But Malledy trusted her about as far as he could throw her. To throw her, however, would require touching her and he was *not* going to make that mistake again. Somehow when they'd been in the woods, she'd been able to slow his heartbeat down to the point that he'd lost consciousness. When his body had fallen away from her touch, her murderous connection was severed or else he would've actually died. Luckily, it was Juliette who'd found his body in the woods. Any other member of Pandora would've likely slit his throat.

Juliette had been extremely angry with Malledy. He'd broken his promises that he would only use her weapon if he was in mortal danger and that he'd never harm the descendant. So, as a consolation, he'd agreed to her plan. Malledy and Juliette would give Pandora's Box back to the Sect if Evangeline agreed to heal him. That meant the slippery freak would have to touch him again. But, this time, if she started humming and pulling that backward song crap she'd pulled on him in the forest, Juliette would be standing by to force Evangeline's hands off him and instantly break the connection. Malledy was confident that the newly converted Evangeline, with her newfound power and purpose, would not risk losing the box. She'd heal Malledy. She had to. He was quite literally betting his life on it.

Once Malledy was cured of Huntington's disease, Juliette believed that they'd race to the airport, take a flight they'd already booked from Portland to Amsterdam, and then fly on to Milan. They'd return to Castle Aertz and to their lives as Archivists, safe inside their ancient, opulent home, surrounded by the knowledge they both craved. But there were a few things she didn't know.

Malledy had been outside Melodie Hopkins' house with his remaining team member, Ivan, when Evangeline had turned the revolver on herself. He'd sent Ivan in to stop her—if she was dead she couldn't cure him. Unfortunately, stupid Ivan had ended up shooting Raphe and getting himself gutted, but Malledy had remained safe, watching the rest of the drama unfold. He'd heard Samantha's words of explanation—the secret about Zeus' curse that only the leaders of Pandora knew and had never written down—and that final secret had truly set him free.

"What do you want?" Evangeline's voice belied her fear.

"Malledy has a fatal illness," Juliette said. "He's got Huntington's disease. It's killing him and we need you to stop its progression and heal him."

"What are you talking about? I don't know how to do that."

"Liar," Malledy said with a sneer. "You healed your little boyfriend." A tremor tore into his left hand and clawed up his arm. With some effort, he pinned his arm against the elevator wall. The spasms were getting much more brutal and his right eye had begun to water and twitch.

Evangeline crossed her arms over her chest. "I don't know how it works."

"You don't need to. I know how it works. I saw it all. Just hum your little song and put your hands on me like you did for Raphe. But if you try to hurt me, like you did before, then we'll take Pandora's Box and sell it to the highest bidder."

"You don't have the box," Evangeline challenged.

"Show her," Malledy said. Juliette held open her purse. Evangeline's eyes grew wide when she saw the golden box inside.

"If you don't heal me, we'll tell the very dangerous men who purchase the box from us exactly where to find you and your friends. Believe me, they won't be as gentle as we're being to you."

"*Arrête,* Malledy," Juliette said, her brow furrowed. "We don't want to hurt you, Evangeline. I have spent my entire life working to protect you for Pandora, but Malledy is my adopted son. *Vous comprenez?*"

"Yes, I think so," Evangeline said.

"Then do it," Malledy demanded.

Chapter Forty-six

Malledy felt the tremors leave his body instantly. His right eye stopped twitching and the dreadful fatigue—that had made him feel like he was slogging through mud carrying one hundred pounds of sand on his back—vanished. It was like he'd been swirling inside a horrendous cyclone and the winds instantly subsided. A white light had enveloped and seeped into him, washing clean his insides which had been so filled with disease and chemicals and stink.

Evangeline was still humming, but Malledy managed to break away from her touch.

"Screw you, Huntington's!" he cried, spinning in a circle, arms raised in triumph. "It's gone, Juliette! It's gone!" He hugged her tightly. "It's gone!"

"Are you truly well?" Juliette asked, pulling back to look into his face.

"Yes," Malledy said. "Yes I am. I'm healed."

"Praise the Gods!" Juliette brushed tears from her eyes. And then she reached over to release the emergency stop button.

Malledy grabbed Juliette's hand. "*Non, ma chere.*" He snatched the purse off her shoulder and pulled out Pandora's Box.

"Evangeline," he said, "open the box for me."

"What?" Evangeline backed away from him, wary as a wildcat. "No way! I made you well—now you're supposed to give *me* the box and leave." She looked to Juliette for confirmation, but the woman was staring at Malledy.

"Are you sure you won't open it for me?" Malledy asked.

"I'm sure," Evangeline said.

Malledy pulled a cruel-looking hunting knife from his jacket pocket. He held it at his side and narrowed his eyes. She'd served her purpose and there was no reason for this girl to suffer too much—he would take her down by cutting the jugular vein. She would be dead in minutes. *I can be benevolent.*

"Malledy, no!" Juliette shrieked. "This is not what we agreed to!"

"That deal was made from a position of weakness. Now I'm strong, so I'm changing the terms. You heard me. I gave Evangeline a chance to open Pandora's Box and live. I am a fair and generous God!"

Juliette's face blanched. "God?"

239

Malledy smiled. "I realized when we were in the woods that there's no longer any difference between me and the Gods and Goddesses whose talismans I've discovered and bent to my will."

"Malledy, I don't understand what you're saying! If you kill Evangeline the box can never be opened. *She's the key.*"

Malledy shook his head. "I know the truth—I heard it with my own ears. Samantha told Evangeline that if she died without having a child, anyone could take the key and open Pandora's Box."

"Maybe that's true," Juliette said in a voice that didn't hide her dread. "I honestly don't know. But if you open the box, Annihilation will be released and people, cities—entire populations will be destroyed. Is that what you really want?"

"Juliette, I'm not just *anyone,* you know. I can use my genius to command the fifth Fury. Controlling Annihilation is the final step in my becoming a modern day God."

"*Mon fils,* I don't understand!" Juliette sounded frightened now. "What's wrong with you?!"

Malledy forced himself to take a calming breath. It wasn't Juliette's fault that she didn't comprehend yet. She was an intellectual, but she wasn't brilliant like him. *She's given me so much and deserves an explanation.*

"At first," Malledy began in a soothing tone, "I thought I'd use the fifth Fury like a scalpel to excise my disease—to literally *annihilate* it. But, now that I'm well, I know that I can do so much more with the final Fury. So much more!"

Malledy took a step toward Evangeline, raising the knife. "Have you watched the news lately, Juliette?"

"*Non.* Malledy, please don't hurt—"

"Shhh. Let me finish explaining," Malledy said gently. "The world is filled with violence, brutality, suicide bombers, massive chemical spills, and nuclear weapons. People are doing exactly what the Gods knew they'd do—destroying each other and destroying their planet without a thought or care. Mankind has no morals and they don't deserve their freedom. Someone needs to control them. Try to understand, Juliette, I didn't ask for this, but it's my destiny. I'm meant to wield Annihilation, the final and most devastating Fury, like a weapon and become the world's tangible God of Knowledge—fair but also too powerful to defy! You see?"

Malledy was so excited, he was spitting each word and saliva coated his chin. "Juliette, people have proven over and over they can't govern themselves. They have to be led, through intellect and violence, when they don't do what's right. I can do that—I can be their God."

Malledy met his mentor's calculating eyes, pleased that their steely resolve had returned. "Juliette, I want *you* to rule beside me. I'll make you a Goddess Mother to humanity just as you were my own adopted mother."

"You're insane," Evangeline hissed. "Totally insane..."

"Shut up!" Malledy commanded. He looked again to Juliette.

A curious smile was spreading across her face. Malledy found it beyond beautiful to behold. *She understands. She's an Archivist first after all.* "So you'll join me?" he asked.

"*Oui,*" Juliette said, stepping forward and wrapping Malledy in a tender embrace.

Evangeline gasped. "What the—?"

Malledy sighed in relief. *Even a God needs company.*

"The end always justifies the means," Juliette whispered in Malledy's ear.

Malledy smiled, and then he felt a sharp and terrible pain in his lower back. The agony was unbearable, unthinkable, undoing all he had planned in one single, horrendous moment. He crumpled to the elevator floor.

"Juliette," he gasped, "what have you done?" Hot blood soaked through his clothing and onto the scuffed white tiles.

Juliette sank down beside Malledy, a bloody stiletto in her hand. "I've saved mankind from you, *mon cher.*"

Malledy's head fell onto Juliette's lap and she rocked him as she'd done when he was a boy scared awake by nightmares.

"It was so very long ago," Malledy murmured, "that you held me like this."

"But I remember," Juliette said. She looked up at Evangeline pressed speechless into the corner of the elevator. "You didn't really heal him, Evangeline."

"What? But, I—I tried to—I think he broke away before it was complete."

Juliette kissed Malledy's ashen face—it was wet from their tears. "I will always love you, *mon fils*."

"I'm *not* your son," Malledy replied.

"But you *are*," Juliette said softly. "Mine and Otto's. That's why you were given a chance to become an Archivist." Malledy's eyes slid closed and his head fell to one side.

Juliette reached up and released the emergency button and then pushed "P3" for the parking garage.

"He wasn't always like this," she told Evangeline. "Once Malledy was a vessel waiting to be filled with knowledge— thirsting for it. He was brilliant and kind and when he smiled... it lit up my heart."

The elevator doors opened in the garage and Juliette handed Evangeline Pandora's Box. "Take it and go!"

Clutching the box, Evangeline stepped out of the elevator and then turned back to face Juliette. "I'm—I'm sorry for... for your loss." The doors closed behind her.

CHAPTER FORTY-SEVEN

The Gods give us small blessings, Juliette thought as the elevator traveled to the roof without stopping to pick up passengers. Her hands and clothes were soaked with blood. Malledy lay dead at her feet. Blood from her single stab wound to his kidney had turned the white floor into a slick ruby pool.

The elevator doors opened.

The sun had risen and it was a cool, clear morning. Gazing out at the mountains in the distance, Juliette thought that there were far worse places. She walked to the edge of the rooftop and looked down at the cars and people twenty stories below. Humanity preserved for yet another day.

Up in the pure blue sky, a falcon was soaring on air currents, his body momentarily blotting out the sun as he circled. Perhaps in death, Malledy had been transformed into this falcon. Perhaps she, too, would be allowed to join him, soaring endlessly—free.

It's a good day to die, Juliette thought. She climbed the low wall encircling the roof. She inhaled deeply, exhaled, and took a step—her eyes trained on the falcon, she plummeted into nothingness.

Chapter Forty-eight

Evangeline sat on a cold concrete barrier in an empty corner of the hospital's parking garage. She was cradling Pandora's Box, which was giving off a soft rose glow. As she traced the intricate swirls carved on its surface, the glow grew stronger.

Turning the box over, she noticed a small keyhole, but she couldn't see a seam where the lid of the box ought to be. She traced the outline of the keyhole and her fingers began to prickle. The onyx key suddenly felt hot and she looked down to see the key straining against its chain, pulling away from her chest, and levitating toward the box.

She pressed the key back against her neck. The desire to take the key off and insert it into the box bloomed in her mind. *Then I will know if all of it is true. And if it isn't, I can go back to who I was, before. I can just be Evangeline Theopolis, without ancient Sects to protect me, or people trying to kill me. If Annihilation isn't in the box, then I'd be truly free.*

The yearning to open the box intensified until it became a steady heartbeat to match her own: *Open it. Open it. Open it.* Evangeline's fingers slid along the chain and she touched the clasp that had previously disappeared. *Sam was wrong—there's one other way it will reappear.* Evangeline pried open the clasp and the key—beautiful and shining despite the dim light—slid into her hand.

Evangeline advanced the key toward the keyhole, which seemed to be drawing it like a powerful magnet. *I can end this nightmare. Maybe once I open the box, I'll wake up at home. Mom will be healthy. Sam will be the godmother I once loved. Melia and Tristin will be alive. I'll be plain old Evangeline again. None of this will have happened. With one turn of the key, I can end the insanity. Open it. Open it. Open it.*

What if it's all true, a tiny voice in the back of Evangeline's mind whispered. *It's not.*

"But what if it is," she asked aloud. *It's not.*

Open it. Open it. Open it.

"What will happen to the people I love if I'm wrong?" *Nothing.*

Open it. Open it. Open it.

"What will happen to the world if I'm wrong?" *Nothing.* NOTHING.

Open it. Open it. Open it.

Evangeline slid the key into the keyhole.

This is as it should be. This is right. This is what the Gods have always wanted. Man must be punished for the crime of accepting fire. I am the key—the key—the key.

"How do I know that I'm the key?" Evangeline whispered.

Because of who you are.

Open it. Open it. Open it.

Every fiber in Evangeline's body was desperate to turn the key, open the box and see what was inside. She was overwhelmed with a burning curiosity—her hands shook with it; her body craved it; the key had to be turned. *This is my destiny. Finally—finally—finally.*

OPEN IT. OPEN IT. OPEN IT!

She began to twist the key…and then she knew—knew without a shadow of a doubt in the way that a person knows if it's day or night.

"I am the descendant of Pandora."

Shutting her eyes, she drew upon strength she'd never known she possessed. She withdrew the key, slid it on the chain, and put the necklace around her neck. As soon as she'd closed the clasp, it disappeared.

"There's no going back."

Feeling exhausted and shaky, Evangeline used the wall behind her to stand and then walked back to the elevator. As she ascended to her mom's floor in safety and silence, she wondered for a brief moment what Juliette had done with Malledy's body. But she didn't dwell on it. That chapter was over. But she knew from this point onward, life was going to be dangerous and deadly—and filled with inexplicable wonders.

Samantha was waiting for Evangeline in the hallway by the bank of elevators. Evangeline handed her Pandora's Box. Sam's expression was a mixture of shock and fear combined with a hard glint in her eyes.

"I'll explain later," Evangeline said. "Right now I just want to sit with my mom." She started to walk away, and then turned. "Samantha, keep the box away from me. Hide it and never let me know where it is. Okay?"

"Why?"

"Because I can't be trusted not to open it." Evangeline met Sam's eyes and an understanding passed between them. "I know who I am now."

And Evangeline walked down the hallway, embracing the uncertainty of her future.

EPILOGUE

The hardest part for Evangeline was the loss of her mother. Her mom would've been able to help her navigate this new life. There were days when the enormity of who she was felt overwhelming. Days when she was totally pissed off that her life wasn't really her own. Days when she felt suffocated by the knowledge that there were people who wanted to kidnap or kill her. Days when the fact that there was a mythic curse hanging over her head felt like a ticking time bomb. And days when she missed her mother and Melia so badly that her heart ached with it.

Dr. Sullivan was a huge help. Maybe it was because they were both going through their own grieving processes. Now that he'd stopped drinking, he'd been forced to deal with his emotions surrounding his wife and daughter's deaths. Evangeline liked to think that she and the doctor could help one and other when the weight of their respective situations got too depressing. Dr. S., as she started to call him, liked to hear her play guitar and sing, so she'd do that for him when he seemed particularly melancholy. And he in turn would get her favorite take-out food (he was a terrible cook), give her driving lessons (he was incredibly calm), and he even helped her turn his daughter's nursery into a fantastic teenager's room.

Dr. S. never forced Evangeline to talk about her feelings—probably because, like her, he needed time and space to process such feelings alone. Dr. S wasn't Evangeline's mom, but for a guardian, he was more than okay.

Rebuilding trust with Samantha was harder than Evangeline had imagined it would be. Wiping the image of Sam suffocating her mom out of her mind was impossible. And her godmother had also kidnapped her and kept her a prisoner. That was tough to forget. But Evangeline was working to forgive Sam. Life was short, especially for a descendant, and she didn't want to spend it weighed down by anger.

It helped to think about all the things that Samantha and the rest of her cult (Evangeline insisted on calling Pandora a cult just to bug her godmother) had sacrificed. Juliette had killed Malledy to save Evangeline and had then taken her own life. Melia had never even *had* her own life before she was struck down saving her. Her best friend had lived with the knowledge that her own mother valued Evangeline's survival over her daughter's, and in the end Melia had died just as she'd always imagined—protecting the descendant. And Samantha and all the leaders before her had never married nor had children, devoting their entire lives to the descendants.

There was a knock on the door.

"Come in," Evangeline called.

Dr. S popped his head in. "You ready E?"

When she turned around, the look on the doctor's face made her blush. "I'm not sure I should let you out of the house," he said.

"We already tried that," Samantha said, walking into the room behind him.

Samantha (her hair chin-length and dyed red) and Dr. S. stared at Evangeline as she smoothed and adjusted her silvery-blue dress, a little uncomfortable with the attention, but also reveling in it. The shimmery sleeveless sheath fell just above Evangeline's knees. Melodie had insisted on sewing the dress for her from a picture Evangeline had torn from W magazine. She'd wanted to make it ankle-length but Evangeline had insisted that shorter was cooler. Dr. Sullivan had suggested sleeves, but Samantha had convinced him otherwise, saying, "Evangeline will make anything she wears look sexy, even if it has a turtleneck, so why not let her have what she wants?"

Evangeline slipped on a pair of high-heeled silver sandals.

"I thought we said one-inch heels," Dr. S. remarked, smiling. He handed her a red leather box with the word *Cartier* in gold script.

"What's this?" Taken aback, Evangeline opened the box. Inside was a pair of delicate platinum and diamond earrings in the shape of flowering vines. They were gorgeous and seemed somehow familiar. She looked at Dr. S., who was studiously cleaning his glasses with the corner of his shirt.

"They were Frances'. She wore them when we got married."

Evangeline remembered now—she'd seen the earrings in the wedding picture on Dr. S.'s refrigerator. "Are you sure?"

"I think she'd want you to have them."

The doorbell rang.

"I'll get that," Dr. S. said, clearly relieved to leave the room.

Evangeline put on the delicate earrings.

"He's doing better," she said to Sam.

"You both are. You look stunning." Sam tucked a curl behind Evangeline's ear. It turned out that Stephanie liked to do hair and she'd somehow tamed Evangeline's wild curls into a loose up-do that accentuated her long neck and showcased the gleaming black key against her skin. "Ready?"

"In a minute. I want to say goodbye to her before I go."

Evangeline walked down the hallway to Dr. S.'s guest room. They'd moved her mother into the house a month ago. She was still breathing on her own, but was what the medical profession called "unresponsive to external stimuli." That basically meant that she remained in a coma, needed a feeding tube, catheter, and to be exercised, massaged, and rolled frequently to prevent bedsores. Samantha and the rest of Pandora had been working in shifts to take care of her—she was one of her own. As for the tumor, it had been slowly and steadily and miraculously shrinking.

Every night Evangeline sat with her mother, reading or singing to her, and telling her about her day. Sometimes she was able to imagine her mother to life for a few moments. But sometimes no matter how hard she tried to imagine her mother into life it didn't work at all, and those days were the hardest because then she was forced to wonder if she'd really done her mom any favors by trying to heal her. Many times she felt like it was arrogance and her own selfish desires that had driven her that day in the hospital. Evangeline knew she would never be certain of her motives. She'd been raw and shell-shocked and desperate.

Evangeline stepped into her mom's room. Her mother looked like a sleeping princess lying in bed covered by her favorite quilt. The swelling had disappeared and, uncharacteristically for a long-term coma patient, she had not curled into a fetal position. Instead, she looked rested—her skin was luminous, her lips rosy, and her hair shiny.

"Hi mom," Evangeline said, taking her hand. She attempted to imagine her mother to life, but when she opened her eyes, her mom was still sleeping. "I'm going to my first prom tonight," Evangeline said. "You'd love my dress. And my heels are so high I'm afraid I might trip. Dr. S. is one of the chaperones. I'm sure there'll be members of the cult lurking around, but I'm getting used to them."

"Evangeline," Dr. Sullivan called. "Raphe's waiting."

"I'll tell you all about it tomorrow," Evangeline promised. She kissed her mom's forehead and walked to the door.

"You look beautiful, honey. My beautiful daughter."

Evangeline whirled around. Her mom was definitely still sleeping, but there was the trace of a smile on her lips. It was something. There was always hope.

ACKNOWLEDGMENTS

Conjuring a story is never done alone. This book was created with the help of my readers: Henry Fischer, Emily Whitfield, Abby Dennis, Ashley Anderson, Colleen Jones, Karen Ford, Kristie Mitchell, Kristin O'Neill, Dan Moretti, Sue Bishop, Jack Bishop, Jax Botterill, Ellen Havdala, and Jane & Art Richardson. All of your comments were helpful and your time was greatly appreciated.

There were two professional editors who helped me along the way. Alix Reid, your focus on story was a perfect match for *Pandora's Key*. Emma Dryden, editor extraordinaire, you helped me take *Pandora's Key* to the next level. I'm so lucky to have you on my team! You rock!!

Many thanks to Amy and Rob Siders at 52 Novels for their hard work on my behalf. And kudos to cover artist Claudia McKinney at Phatpuppy Art for her incredible cover.

Most of all, this book couldn't have been written without the support of my husband, Henry, who believes in me. H, I love you the whole world round and back again!

ABOUT THE AUTHOR

Nancy Richardson Fischer lives in Oregon with her husband, Henry, and their Vizsla, Boone. When she's not conjuring a story, she's kite-boarding, biking, skiing and planning adventures with her family.

Visit: NancyRichardsonFischer.com to learn about other books published by this author, and to read the first chapter in *The Key to Tartarus*, The Key Trilogy – Book Two.

More by This Author

Feel No Fear: The Power, Passion and Politics of a Life in Gymnastics, with Bela Karolyi

Riding For My Life, with Julie Krone

Monica: From Fear to Victory, with Monica Seles

Winning Every Day, with Shannon Miller

A Journey: The Autobiography of Apolo Anton Ohno, with Apolo Anton Ohno

Nadia Comaneci: Letters to a Young Gymnast, with Nadia Comaneci

The Golden Globe (Star Wars Junior Jedi Knights)

Lyric's World (Star Wars Junior Jedi Knights)

Promises (Star wars Junior Jedi Knights)

Coming Soon From

NANCY RICHARDSON FISCHER

THE KEY TO TARTARUS

THE KEY TRILOGY • BOOK TWO

PROLOGUE

Before the Greek Gods of Mount Olympus there were the Titans, a race of powerful deities that ruled the cosmos. Cronus, the Titans' king, was warned by a soothsayer that one of his children would someday overthrow him. So he swallowed each of his first five children right after they were born. Cronus' wife, distraught at the loss of her babies, devised a plan to save her sixth child. When her son Zeus was born, she wrapped a stone in baby blankets and presented it to her husband. Oblivious to his wife's trickery, Cronus didn't check inside the blanket and swallowed the stone instead of his son.

Zeus was hidden from Cronus until he was strong enough to overthrow his father's rule. Conspiring with his mother, he dressed as a servant and gave his father a poison elixir that caused him to vomit out his five children—including

Zeus' brothers, Poseidon and Hades. The siblings joined together to overthrow Cronus and the Titans in a bloody, ten-year war. Once victorious, Zeus and his brothers imprisoned Cronus and the rest of the Titans in Tartarus—a terrible dungeon deep beneath the underworld from which there was no escape.

Following the war, Zeus, Poseidon and Hades divided up rule of the cosmos. Because Zeus had saved his siblings' lives, he was given first choice and chose to be named King of the Greek Gods. Armed with powerful lightning bolts he ruled over the sky from Mount Olympus. Poseidon was given rule of the sea armed with a magical trident he could use to create calm waters or strike when angered to cause earthquakes and massive tidal waves. Hades was left to oversee the Underworld, rich with gold, silver and precious stones but also a dark realm of despair created to house the souls of the dead.

None of the brothers ever imagined that mankind might evolve and no longer believe or pray to the Greek Gods, instead trusting in their own abilities to control the universe. And most certainly they could never have imagined that when men discarded their beliefs it would cause some Gods' powers to wane and eventually all but fade from the universe.

But a forgotten God is a vengeful God; such a God will commit heinous crimes to regain their power and display their wrath.

PART ONE

CHAPTER ONE

.... Evangeline blushed and stared down at the book. "Okay, what are we reading about today?"

"Tartarus," Edwall said with a grin.

"Who's Tartarus?" Raphe asked, perching on the window-sill, his skateboard at his feet.

"Not who. What. And you'll see soon enough." Edwall clapped his hands like an excited child. "Start reading, Evangeline. Pretty please."

Evangeline began to read: "Below the underworld is an infernal dungeon called Tartarus."

"I wouldn't even think of going there," Edwall cautioned Evangeline, his light-gray eyes twinkling beneath overgrown silver brows.

"Why not? It sounds like the perfect place for a vacation."

"Because Tartarus is despair," the old man replied with a grimace. "It's an abyss to house the souls of the damned and the dead. Tartarus is hell times infinity and there's no escape... Melia is there, you know."

The skin on the back of Evangeline's neck prickled. *How did Edwall know Melia's name? And why would he think her best friend was in some mythical dungeon?* "Um, how could you—I don't think—"

"She's suffering every moment of every day for eternity for the sin of betraying the descendant of Pandora."

"That's ridiculous," Evangeline blurted out. *Why am I even getting upset? I don't believe in Tartarus or anything else in the old guy's book. But how does he know Melia's name?*

"Malledy is probably there, too," the old man continued as Raphe hopped off the windowsill and moved toward Evangeline. Edwall licked his chapped lips and blinked several times. His eye color shifted from washed-out gray to a deep slate. He winked at Raphe. "You wanna see your old buddy?"

CPSIA information can be obtained at www.ICGtesting.com
Printed in the USA
LVOW041724080612

285296LV00001B/113/P